HEARTSIDE BAY

THE **HEARTSIDE BAY** SERIES

HEARTSIDE BAY

A
Date
With
Fate

CATHY COLE

SCHOLASTIC

With many thanks to Lucy Courtenay and Sara Grant

Scholastic Children's Books
An imprint of Scholastic Ltd
Euston House, 24 Eversholt Street, London, NW1 1DB, UK
Registered office: Westfield Road, Southam, Warwickshire, CV47 0RA
SCHOLASTIC and associated logos are trademarks and/or
registered trademarks of Scholastic Inc.

First published in the UK by Scholastic Ltd, 2014

Text copyright © Scholastic Ltd, 2014

ISBN 978 1407 14049 0

A CIP catalogue record for this book
is available from the British Library.

Printed by CPI Group (UK) Ltd, Croydon, CR0 4YY
Papers used by Scholastic Children's Books are made
from wood grown in sustainable forests.

3 5 7 9 10 8 6 4 2

www.scholastic.co.uk

(This dedication was donated by the author)

To our lovely Grace,
you are our sunshine.
Mum, Dad, Ellie, Emily and Andrew

ONE

Eve Somerstown fiddled with the buttons on her seat, enjoying the way the mechanism moved her chair smoothly to the perfect position. Stretching out her toes, she admired her new shoes, turning her feet so the lights caught the gold bars on the strappy red sandals and made them gleam. She flicked through the channels on the TV in front of her, sighed, and turned it off.

Even private jets can be boring when there's no one to talk to, she thought.

Eve's stomach twisted in the usual way. No one was talking to her right now anyway. Even if her friends had been right here on the plane, she knew they would all have their backs to her.

Turning her head, she looked at her shopping bags

with their familiar Paris logos and expensive rope handles. The sight soothed her, and excitement fluttered in her stomach. She had bought some gorgeous things on this trip. She couldn't wait to try them on again in front of the long, adjustable three-way mirror in her bedroom.

How does anyone live with one flat mirror? she wondered, pulling a little sea-blue sequinned dress from a bag and holding it up to the light, making it sparkle like the bars on her sandals. Everyone knew that a new dress had to look good from the back as well as the front.

Laying the dress on the empty white-leather seat beside her and reaching for a baby-blue-and-white striped bag with gold tasselled handles, Eve pulled out her favourite purchase. Soft as down and the most delectable shade of purple, the cashmere wrap felt as warm as a mother's embrace.

Eve's mother didn't hug her much, admittedly. But Eve knew what it felt like. She snuggled her nose into the fluff and breathed its lovely new smell. Then she stroked the cashmere, folded it, and laid it gently on top of the sparkling dress.

Her dad laid down his phone and flicked through the winking tablet on the table in front of him, his long fingers moving with speed and assurance. No one could deny that Henry Somerstown was a handsome man who looked ten years younger than his age. Eve hoped her husband would age as well as her dad had. Swirling his sparkling water gently in its glass, Eve's father glanced at her as if he had just remembered she was there. "How are you doing over there, baby girl?"

Eve snatched the moment. "Isn't this the most beautiful thing you've ever seen, Daddy?" she said, quickly holding up the sea-blue dress for her father to admire. The cashmere slithered to the carpeted floor. "They only had one left and it was in my size, can you believe it? I was totally meant to have it. I—"

The phone started purring. Eve's father lifted a hand apologetically, and took the call. "Mr Hong, great to hear from you. Safe trip home from Shanghai?"

Eve lowered her dress and stared out of the window, determined not to mind. It was her dad's business that had brought her to Paris in the first place, after all. She had no right to begrudge him a few business calls. She would give him a proper fashion show when they got home.

Eve bit her lip in vexation, remembering that her sister would probably be at home. Chloe knew how to wind

Eve up by dancing around their dad and tugging on his hands and talking in the special baby voice that she put on just for him. Their dad fell for it every single time. Eve was as good as invisible the moment Chloe skipped into the room.

Eve took up the cashmere wrap again, from where it had slipped on to the floor. It was already losing its feeling of newness, and she saw that it had snagged on one of the sea-blue dress's sharp blue sequins. She threw it down in frustration.

Daddy loves me, she told herself. *He wouldn't have brought me on this trip otherwise.* Did he love her more than Chloe? She had never dared to ask.

"Yes, everything's on track, Mr Hong." Her dad's Rolex glinted in the private jet's discreet overhead lights as he checked the time and glanced out of the window at the approaching lights of the English coast. "The units are being snapped up so fast, I can hardly keep up with demand. We have some big-name labels moving into the centre as soon as the space is habitable. It's going to be extremely profitable. Worth every penny we've put into it so far, I would say. Your investment will double by the time I've finished with the Heartside Shopping Centre."

Her dad only had to look at a project and it turned to gold, Eve thought, determined to cheer herself up. The designer names that had said they'd take a unit in his new shopping development were the best in the world. He was the most important man in Heartside Bay, and he was brilliant at his job. He knew everyone, had great parties, and loved her to pieces.

She breathed in the cashmere one more time, then dropped it carelessly back into its blue and white bag.

"Not long to go before we land," said Eve's dad, slotting his phone into his pocket. "Have you enjoyed yourself today, Evie? I'm sorry I couldn't come to the shops with you."

"It's OK, Daddy," said Eve in a rush of love. "Your business always has to come first, I understand that. I'm fifteen now, I can look after myself. Paris was gorgeous. It's so beautiful at this time of year."

"I'm sorry Rhi couldn't come to keep you company," her dad said. "I haven't seen her around much recently. Is she still busy with her singing?"

Eve felt her chin start to wobble. Her dad looked surprised and concerned.

"Everything OK, baby girl?"

For one weak moment, Eve wanted to pour out all her problems. Tell her dad everything that had been going wrong in her life lately. The new girl Lila Murray stealing Ollie, the boy Eve had chosen for herself. The horrible mess-up with Rhi and Max. Eve wasn't even sure why she'd bothered to go after Max in the first place. She didn't even like him that much. Now Rhi hated Eve for trying to steal him, and Max had ended up going back to Rhi anyway. Even Polly Nelson thought she was evil, and Eve had been trying to do Polly and her mum a favour when she'd sorted out that problem with Ms Andrews! She'd saved Ms Andrews from losing her job after she'd started dating Polly's mum. Her stomach clenched at the thought of that particular conversation. She'd never make *that* mistake again. And after everything, Eve just wasn't sure who she was any more. Nothing seemed right.

Your dad has more important things to think about than your little problems, Eve reminded herself. *He deserves a happy daughter, not a miserable one.*

But the words started tumbling out before she could stop herself.

"Well, there have been a couple of things at school lately. Boys, friends. You know."

She bit her lip before she said anything more. Her dad would be so disappointed in her if he knew everything that was going wrong. She couldn't tell him.

"But it's nothing I can't handle," she added quickly.

Giving her father her most dazzling smile, she flicked her long auburn hair back over her shoulders. He laughed, and relaxed back against his chair.

"You know what I think?"

He had a teasing tone in his voice that made Eve sit upright.

"I think," he said, "that it's time for another one of your amazing parties. My princess is always happiest when she's party planning. Am I right?"

Eve squealed and jumped out of her chair to give her dad a hug. Parties were her favourite thing. When she was hosting a party, nothing else seemed to matter. Her mind had already started whirling through themes, guest lists and outfits.

"Brilliant!" she gasped. "My last party was at home, so I think we should go somewhere else this time. Can I hire a venue?"

"Name it," said her father.

Eve sat beside him, her eyes glowing with ideas. "How

about one of the little islands off the coast? We can bring people over on the yacht. The weather at this time of year will be perfect! We'll have a striped beach marquee, and a barbecue. No, wait! A fire pit! We can have a Caribbean theme!" She could picture it already. "There'll be flares along the shore and a live band. It'll be by invitation only, of course. All the best parties are."

"It already sounds legendary," laughed her dad. "Who will you invite?"

Eve thought of Lila and Ollie, Rhi and Max, and Polly. She had a nasty feeling none of them would want to come.

"Only the best," Eve said defiantly.

I'll just have to make it extra amazing, she thought fiercely. *Then they won't be able to say no.*

Eve settled back into her chair and clipped her seat belt together, dreaming of the perfect evening that she was going to host. It would be the best party ever.

Her dad's phone rang. He stared at the number on the screen and snatched it up.

"Talk to me," he said.

Eve couldn't hear what the person on the other end was saying, but the voice sounded anxious. Her father's face grew thunderous.

"Sort it out, Monroe," he snapped. "I can't have this. Do your job, or I'll have to find someone else to do it for you. Do I make myself clear?"

Eve refolded her new clothes dreamily, running through the party order in her mind.

"Damn it Monroe! This is going to set us back weeks, if not months. Do you have any idea how much a delay like this will cost me?"

Her dad's voice was rising. He could be really fierce sometimes, Eve thought, feeling a little sorry for the person on the other end of the phone.

Eve's dad loosened his tie with a quick, angry movement. "If this isn't sorted by the weekend, it's not just your neck that will be on the line, Monroe. You'll be hearing from me. This isn't the last of it."

To Eve's astonishment, her dad threw his phone down so hard that it bounced off the seat to the floor. From the sound of things, there was a serious problem.

Eve dismissed the thought as soon as she'd had it. There couldn't be a problem. Her dad was always a success. Everyone knew that.

TWO

Eve fiddled with the new gold watch she'd bought in Paris. It had looked so good on her wrist in the shop. Now in the harsh light of the classroom it looked cheap.

She assessed the boys in the classroom. If her island beach party was going to be a success, she needed a date. And it had to be a good one. The best guy in the room.

Ollie Wright's handsome blond head was bent towards Lila Murray's glossy brown one, and he was laughing at something she was saying. Eve felt the old, familiar wave of anger. *She* was supposed to date the most popular boy, not Lila. Now it would probably never happen. Not for the first time, Eve wished Lila had never arrived in Heartside Bay and disrupted her carefully laid plans. Anyone with half a brain could see how perfect Eve and Ollie would look together.

Max Holmes was another no. *Been there, done that*, Eve thought, unmoved as he ran his hands lazily through his thick dark hair and gave her what he thought was his most seductive wink. *And you were a lot more trouble than you were worth*.

Ryan Jameson was resting his chin on the desk, gazing surreptitiously at Lila through his overgrown fringe. *Another one with a crush on the new girl*, thought Eve with extreme irritation. Ryan was much too annoying for date material. And as for the rest of the boys in 10Y, they were all the same loud, annoying, stupid kids she'd been at school with for ever, and none of them had improved with the passing years.

She paused when she reached Josh Taylor. Now here was someone who *had* improved, she realized. Josh had always been the gawky nerd in the corner, doodling in his sketchbook and never saying a word to anyone. He still wasn't the world's greatest conversationalist, but his shoulders had broadened nicely, and his short hair and dorky glasses had actually become somewhat stylish.

Sensing her gaze, Josh turned and glanced at her, his green eyes enquiring. Eve felt a jolt of excitement. Josh was smart and good-looking. She'd never known him to have a girlfriend, now she thought about it. He was a bit of a man of mystery, which added to his appeal.

Could she fall for him?

Eve wasn't sure she'd ever really fallen for anybody. She'd had boyfriends, always good-looking ones, but once the thrill of the chase had passed, she always found herself losing interest. She had long ago decided that the spark she'd heard about in love songs was a myth. Love was about making the most advantageous choices, that was all.

What's not to like with Josh? she asked herself, studying the back of his bent head, imagining the way his close-cut hair might feel under her fingers. She could make him like her, she was sure of it. And she could learn to like him too. She could make it work.

There was no time like the present to start her flirt campaign. She would play this just right. Josh would be her prize.

The bell rang for the end of class. Snatching up her

bag, Eve walked up to Josh, pushing past the other students to make sure she was in the perfect position to strike up a corridor conversation.

"Hey Josh," she said in her most flirtatious voice.

Josh glanced at her in surprise. Making a show of adjusting his bag on his shoulder, he pushed his glasses up his nose. "Hey," he said awkwardly.

Eve smiled up at him. He was lovely and tall. This plan was getting better by the minute.

"You were looking very studious in there," she teased, wrinkling her nose at him. "I don't know how you can concentrate in that bear pit."

"Oh, you know," said Josh, with a shrug. "I'm pretty used to the bears by now."

Eve fluttered her eyelashes. Just a little. She didn't want to be too obvious. "So," she said in her most thoughtful voice. "Am I one of the bears?"

"I'd call you more of a tiger."

For a moment, Eve felt unsure of herself. "I'm not sure whether that's a good thing or not," she said, forcing a little laugh.

Josh looked alarmed. "I'm sorry, I didn't mean to insult you or anything. I . . . just wasn't expecting the question. Zoology isn't really my area."

Eve laughed for real this time. She added "funny" to the growing list of Josh Taylor's attractions.

"Tigers are prettier than bears, I suppose," she said with a carefully measured pout.

"Definitely," Josh agreed, looking relieved that she hadn't taken offence.

Eve ran her fingers through her hair. Boys always found her hair fascinating. Sure enough, she saw Josh's eyes flicker. "And I have more tigerish colouring," she mused, pleased with the effect she was creating.

"Unless you count the auburn-haired bears of Bolivia."

"There are auburn-haired bears in Bolivia?" Eve said, startled by the serious look on Josh's face.

It was Josh's turn to laugh this time. "Just kidding."

Eve wasn't sure whether she was being laughed at. Taking a deep breath, she gave him her most dazzling smile.

"And is my roar worse than my bite?" she said coquettishly.

"I wouldn't know," Josh said, smiling back. "I haven't been roared at yet."

They turned a corner towards the maths block. And Eve spotted the last person in the world that she wanted to see.

"Hi Josh!" Lila gave Eve a wary nod. "Eve."

"Lila," said Eve stiffly.

Josh beamed at Lila. "How's it going?"

"Fantastic, thanks," said Lila, giving Josh a warm smile. "You know, for a Monday morning. What are you two talking about?"

"Bears and tigers, mostly," said Josh.

"Nutter," said Lila, laughing.

Eve realised with some horror that Josh's ears had turned pink. It was suddenly as clear as crystal why Josh was permanently single. The girl he liked was already spoken for.

Josh liked Lila.

Eve wanted to stamp on Lila's foot. First Ollie, then Ryan, now Josh! How come she got all the boys' attention? She wasn't even that pretty. OK, she was, but there were more beautiful girls at Heartside High.

Eve put her arm possessively through the crook of Josh's elbow. He looked a little startled, but didn't pull away.

"This chit-chat is all very nice," she said waspishly, "but we have a class to get to. Shall we keep walking?"

Lila grinned. "How stupid of me to forget," she said. She gave a little bow, extending her hand in front of Eve. "After you, your Royal Highness."

Eve raged internally all the way to maths, practically towing Josh beside her like a dog on a lead. Lila Murray wanted to play, did she? Well, this time the new girl didn't stand a chance.

THREE

Eve ate lunch as quickly as she could. At a table near the door, Josh was finishing off a sandwich and packing up his bag. The moment he left the canteen, Eve followed as closely as she dared.

A number of kids left the school building in lunch break. Eve blended in with the crowd jostling through the double doors. Josh was already some way ahead of her, his long legs striding easily down the steps outside the school building and away down the high street.

Eve snatched a quick glimpse of herself in a shop window. There was no point in any of this if she didn't look good. The warm breeze had brought a flush of colour to her pale cheeks, but her lips were dry and her hair a little messy. She could live with the hair, Eve decided, but had to sort her lips out. Boys liked soft, inviting lips. She whipped out her favourite gloss and applied it with a swift one-two swipe of the wand. Much better.

To her dismay, when she looked ahead again, she realized Josh had vanished. Eve jogged up and down the high street, peering inside the shops and checking her gold watch, feeling jumpy. Time was passing too fast for comfort. Soon she'd have to be back in class. Where had he disappeared to?

Eve turned off the high street, feeling a little desperate. The sea wind hit her head-on, blowing her hair right back from her face. To her relief, she spotted Josh sitting on the beach, his rucksack by his side and his head bent over something.

Making a mental note to keep her face to the wind – strands of hair sticking to lip gloss was not a good look – Eve straightened her shoulders and strode over.

Josh was drawing. Eve stopped in the sand and gazed over his shoulder as his pencil drew the swift outline of a gull banking over the sand, flight feathers outstretched like fingers. It was so lifelike, she half-expected it to fly off the page with its usual seaside shriek. She was genuinely impressed.

There was a portrait of a laughing girl on the facing page. Eve had hardly glimpsed it when Josh flipped the sketchbook to a clean page – but she'd seen enough to recognise the face.

Lila Murray again.

When would Lila stop getting in the way?

I knows more ways to snag a boy than you've ever dreamed of, new girl, she thought, feeling the fierce flush of competition rush through her blood. *By the time I've finished with Josh, he'll be putty in my hands.*

Eve knew exactly how to hook someone like Josh. Scratch the surface on any boy, cool guy or geeky nerd, and they were all the same. If you played it right, in no time at all the boys rolled at your feet like puppies begging to have their tummies tickled. It was pathetic really.

Rule number one: compliment them.

"That's an amazing seagull," she said warmly. She didn't even have to fake it. He really was good. "You're properly talented, Josh."

Josh closed his sketchbook, clearly surprised to see Eve standing there. "Thanks," he said. "What are you doing out here?"

Eve knew the rules as well as if she'd had them tattooed on the insides of her eyelids. *Rule number two*: *add a little mystery.*

She turned to face the waves, taking care to pull her hair well back from her lips. "I like to think out here sometimes," she said in her most serious voice. "School can get a little too . . . intense. The sea makes everything clearer."

"I find that too," he said, looking interested.

Boys were so predictable. The puppy-tummy stage was already only a few steps away.

"Can I sit with you?" she asked, flicking her eyes sideways at him.

Josh laid out his coat so she wouldn't have to sit on the sand and patted the space. "Best view in the house," he said.

It *was* a great view, the way the waves curled and dashed themselves against the sand. There was something mesmerizing about it. If it weren't for the fact that Eve was losing the battle between her hair and the wind, she would have almost said she was enjoying herself.

Rule number three, she thought. *Ask questions. A*

LOT of questions.

"Do you come out here a lot?"

He nodded, opening up his sketchbook again. "All the time."

Eve shifted so she was looking directly into his eyes. They were lovely eyes. Bright green eyes. She put her whole soul into her next question.

"What makes this place special for you?"

Josh fiddled with his sketchpad, and Eve felt a little flicker of pleasure. He couldn't hold her gaze. She'd work on that. Coax him gently into the sunlight. Let him know that it was OK to look as long as he liked.

"Probably the same thing that makes it special for you," he replied. His head was bent over the page, his pencil making swift marks on the page. "The peace of it. The grandeur."

Grandeur was a nice word. Eve liked it. She nudged very gently against his shoulder. "What are you drawing now?"

"Something I've been working on for a while." He flushed, looking nervous suddenly. "Do you want to see?"

She put her hand on his arm. "I'd love to see

anything you want to show me, Josh."

He fumbled a little, opening up the sketchbook. Eve stared at the little panels, the word bubbles, the energy of the pictures. "You're drawing a comic book?" she said.

"A graphic novel," he said a little tightly, and shut the sketchbook with a final-sounding slam.

Eve realized that she was pushing this too fast. Josh would wriggle off her hook if she didn't tread carefully. She changed tack.

"I didn't know there was a difference," she said quickly. "I don't know anything about graphic novels. I didn't mean any offence."

She gazed at her hands in what she hoped was a suitably humble kind of way, waiting and hoping for the moment when Josh would relax again.

"Comic books are for kids," he said after a moment. "Graphic novels are on a different level. I'll show you what I mean."

He got his sketchbook out again, opening it up to a central page covered in strong dark lines. Eve felt a wave of relief. She hadn't lost her fish yet.

As Josh explained the concept behind his graphic

novel – something about a quest in a magical land – Eve mentally constructed the perfect wardrobe for him to wear to her party. It would have to match her dress, but not in an obvious way. It was all about getting the right feeling. A touch of blue somewhere. Maybe on his socks?

"What do you think?" Josh was looking at her expectantly. Eve blinked, caught off guard.

"I agree!" she fudged with a little laugh.

He looked a little confused. "I asked what you thought about graphic-novel heros needing a dark past."

Oops. Eve's eyes darted towards the tall figure in the billowing black cloak standing in the central panel Josh had been showing her. The guy did look pretty dark. Right?

"I meant, I agree they *should* have a dark past!" She threw in a pout, just in case.

Josh looked back at his sketchbook. "Just as well," he said a little drily. "I don't think my guy has too many memories of kittens and snowballs."

This wasn't going quite as smoothly as Eve had hoped. Time to ramp it up a little. Reaching over, she placed her hand lightly on his arm.

"You've caught the dark thing really well, Josh," she said seriously. "I think you are brilliant at what you do. To be honest, I'm a little dazzled. Do you have a publishing deal?"

He looked wistful. "As if. I'm only at the preliminary stages."

Eve squeezed his arm through his sleeve. "Daddy knows heaps of people in publishing," she said firmly. "We'll get him to call someone to take a look. This deserves to be published."

Josh's eyes widened. "Are you serious?"

Daddy knows lots of people, Eve thought. *There's bound to be a few publishers in the mix.* She was never one to let truth get in the way of a conquest. "I've never been more serious in my life," she said.

Josh looked even more handsome when he was happy. "That's amazing, Eve," he stammered. "You . . . you're amazing."

Eve gave him her sweetest smile, cocking her head. "It's your talent, Josh," she said honestly. "I'm just the facilitator."

"Stay still," he said suddenly, scrabbling in his

pocket. "I'm going to draw you. I can put you in the novel if you want."

Eve's heart jumped. "You want to draw me?"

"Drawing you already. Keep your head still."

Josh's fingers were flying over the sketch pad, shading and sketching, outlining and cross-hatching, until a figure emerged on the page.

Josh flipped the pad round to show her. "You like it?"

Eve wasn't sure she recognized herself. The girl Josh had drawn was strong and beautiful with lustrous hair and big eyes, in a kind of sleek body armour that hugged the curves of her body. She liked it. If she could just feel like that inside, she thought wistfully, she could conquer the world.

Josh flipped the sketch pad shut. "It's just a sketch," he said shyly. "I'll work it up into something better for next time."

Eve stared into his green eyes. He was amazing. He was perfect for her in every way. How had she never seen it before? She *had* to snare him. Right now.

She cast her mind back to rule number three. *Ask questions.*

"So Josh," she said, keeping her expression as warm

and inviting as she could. "Where do you live?"

Josh slid his sketchbook into his bag. "In the old town."

Eve felt excited. She'd never met anyone who actually lived in the old town before, with its ancient, salt-stained buildings and dark, cobbled lanes. "How cute!" she said warmly. "In one of the old fishing cottages? I bet your mother has done the most amazing things to it. Those little places look so charming."

Josh yanked his jacket from beneath her so quickly that Eve almost fell backwards.

"You should try living in one," he said, standing up. "Better get back to school or we'll be late."

"But. . ."

He was striding up the beach already, his head tucked down into the collar of his jacket and his arms wrapped around his bag. Getting to her feet and hurrying after him, Eve felt as if more than a jacket had been pulled from underneath her. The sand itself felt a little unsteady.

Had she ruined it with Josh already?

FOUR

The rest of the afternoon was lonely.

Josh had only returned Eve's smile once during afternoon classes, and ducked his head down again straight afterwards. It was extremely vexing. If Eve had blown her chances with the only guy in class worth her time and effort . . . well. It didn't bear thinking about what that said about her.

As for her former friends, they were all doing a good job of ignoring her. Lila, Polly, Rhi, Ollie. Even Max's eyes had slid away from her after class, despite Eve shooting him her most inviting smile. She was used to being invisible at home, but this was a different matter. School was Eve's kingdom. No one ignored her at school.

I have to figure out a way to get back on top, she thought, packing away her books more fiercely than necessary at the end of class.

No one was waiting for her, the way they usually did. No one at all. Acting as though it didn't matter in the least, Eve shouldered her bag and left the school building with her head held high and thought about the problem.

Daddy says there's no such things as problems, she reminded herself as she marched along the high street. *Only solutions no one's thought of yet.*

And almost at once, the perfect solution came to her, blowing down the street with the leaves and the litter. Eve stopped, dazzled by her own brilliance.

Changing direction, she hurried towards her father's gleaming beachside office. The tips of the waves were whiter and frothier than than they had been at lunch, and the gulls were struggling to fly in a straight line. Eve didn't notice. She took the lift to the top floor to give herself a chance to catch her breath and check her reflection in the lift mirror. The wind had brightened her cheeks nicely.

Her father's suite of offices were bright and modern,

humming with activity and the sound of rapid typing. Eve strode across the soft carpet to her dad's secretary's desk.

"Is Daddy free, Gloria? I have something really important that I want to ask him."

Gloria peered at Eve over the top of her gold spectacle frames. "Hello to you too, Eve," she said in her dry Scottish accent. "Your father's extremely busy today, but I'll let him know you're here. If you'd like to take a seat?"

Eve flung herself down into a big leather armchair her dad used for guests, and stared out of the windows, tapping her fingernails impatiently on the armrest. She could see the shopping centre from here. It looked as if it was almost finished.

Her father's office door opened.

"This is a nice surprise, Eve," said her dad. "To what do I owe this pleasure?"

Eve jumped up and hugged her father affectionately. His hair looked extra-rumpled today, and his eyes were tired.

"You need a holiday, Daddy," Eve said, looking up at him with concern.

Her father seemed distracted. "Be quick, Evie. I have a hundred things to do."

"I know you do, Daddy," Eve soothed. "But I just have a teensy favour I want to ask you."

"Eve," he said warningly, "I have a lot—"

"I'll do everything," Eve said quickly, before she lost his attention. "But I just need your permission."

"Permission for what?"

Eve beamed. "To host a school trip to the office! It would be brilliant for everyone to see what you do here. It fits in really well with our careers training, and it would raise your profile and the profile of the new shopping centre. You're always saying how important it is to do that, right?"

She could see the whole day in her mind's eye already. Activities for her classmates, a project for them all to work on back in the classroom. It would impress everyone – not least of all Josh. She had a particular job in mind for Josh, a job that would prove how much she had been thinking about him and his career.

"We'll fit it in with you, of course." Eve's mind was whirring at a hundred miles an hour through the endless benefits a trip like this would bring her. "But I was thinking we could do it next week?"

"You have a lot of appointments next week, Mr Somerstown," Gloria called from behind her desk. "There's hardly any space at all for an event on the scale your daughter is proposing."

Gloria could be a real killjoy sometimes, Eve thought. Couldn't the old trout see how good this would be?

"I'd just need a list of the businesses who are buying units in the shopping centre, Daddy," she said, determined not to be thwarted. "I'll plan the whole event down to the last paper clip. And I thought maybe you could give a talk as well? We'll focus the trip on retailing and branding, and you'd be the perfect speaker because you're so brilliant at it."

"Mr Somerstown, I—" Gloria began.

"Thank you, Gloria," Mr Somerstown interrupted, raising his hand. "We can fit my daughter in somewhere, I'm sure. How about Wednesday?"

Eve gave Gloria her sunniest smile.

If anything, the old secretary looked more irritated than ever. "As you wish, Mr Somerstown," she said tightly.

"Wednesday it is, then," said Mr Somerstown, tapping Eve on the end of her nose. "And with my little girl in charge, I know it'll be the best school trip in the world."

"Are you ready?" said Josh, staring into Eve's eyes.

"Ready is a state of mind, Josh," Eve said. "And I am *always* ready."

It had been the busiest week and a half Eve had ever known. She'd loved every minute. Calling the shopping centre's future businesses and coaxing free gifts out of them for the goodie bags. Organizing the afternoon's activities. Designing the logo for the day. OK, so Josh had done the designing – and he'd done an incredible job, as Eve had known he would. But there was no escaping the fact that this whole day was down to her.

The Queen Bee was back.

"Then if you're ready," said Josh, interrupting Eve's pleasant train of thought, "take it away."

The noise of 10Y chattering in the downstairs reception area of Somerstown Developments was tremendous. Eve tugged her blazer into place, clapped her hands and raised her voice.

"Hello everyone, and welcome!"

Everyone quietened and faced her. Eve relished the way Rhi, Polly and Lila's eyes were, finally, fixed entirely on her. At the way Josh was standing by her side.

"I can't thank you enough for coming," she said warmly. "I'm sure we'll all learn something new, and take away some great memories. Take the lifts to the top floor, or the stairs if you want a little exercise. Let's have some fun!"

Hosting an away day was just the same as hosting a party, Eve decided happily as they took the lifts and emerged in the top-floor offices of Somerstown Developments. No wonder she was so good at it.

"Help me to sort out the goodie bags, Josh," she suggested. "Girls' bags are in the first box, boys' bags in the second."

Josh stared at the boxes stacked by the office door. "There are different ones?"

"I don't suppose you've noticed," Eve said patiently, "but girls and boys are entirely different species. Of *course* the bags are different. Goodie bags, everyone!"

The bags contained all the freebies Eve had sourced

from the shopping centre's future businesses: hair accessories, beauty products and purses for the girls; gadgets, pens and headphones for the boys. There were T-shirts too, emblazoned with Josh's logo for the day: a heart shape containing the words ALL YOUR HEARTSIDE'S DESIRE in a cool font. The logo was on the bags themselves as well.

"You've thought of everything, haven't you?" Josh said.

"Everything apart from a tour of the shopping centre," Eve said with a sigh. "That would have been perfect, but even I couldn't make it happen."

She had tried every trick she could think of to wangle a tour of the building site, but to no avail. The excuses had been a mile long from everyone she had contacted.

"Still," she said, straightening her shoulders, "the best party hosts should always be flexible."

Josh shook his head. "You really are amazing."

"I think you bring out the best in me, Josh," Eve said, and patted his hand.

When he didn't snatch his hand away, she felt a warm tingle of anticipation in her belly. She almost had him. She was sure of it.

The goodie bags were an instant hit with the class.

"Nice," said Lila, tugging out her T-shirt and holding it up against herself. "And these are really all free? You're something else, Eve."

"I love it!" said Rhi as she slid a new hairclip into her thick dark hair.

"You've done really well, Eve," said Polly.

Eve had been longing to hear kind words like these from her friends for ages. "Thanks," she said, forcing back the tears that had made a sudden and unwelcome appearance in the back of her eyes.

Her heart skipped as her father came out of his office. There was no sign of tiredness or stress today. He was wearing his best suit, his Rolex gleaming on his wrist. She felt so proud of him, she thought she might burst.

"On behalf of us all, Mr Somerstown," said her form teacher, Mr Morrison, warmly, "we'd like to say a huge thank you for allowing us the use of your offices and your staff today. We are so grateful for the opportunity to visit you here."

"Hear, hear," shouted Ollie Wright. Eve noticed he was wearing his T-shirt over his school uniform.

Mr Somerstown raised his hands to silence the burst of applause. "Thank you for coming. I'm delighted to offer you something to commemorate the first Somerstown Developments Business Away Day we have ever had. Here's to more in the future."

Gloria produced a small wooden shield emblazoned with Josh's logo, which Mr Somerstown presented to Mr Morrison. Underneath were the words: *For 10Y, the Future of Heartside Bay. Warmest regards, Somerstown Developments.*

Eve's heart swelled with pride as Mr Morrison accepted the shield with a surprised smile.

"There's one more thing before we move on to today's activities," said Mr Somerstown. He moved over to a small blue curtain on one wall. "I'm delighted to present to you a list of Somerstown Developments' investors. I am sure you will recognize a good many names on this list. It is down to their generosity that Heartside Bay will soon have the retail centre that it needs and deserves. We're putting the finishing touches to the complex as I speak."

At the tug of a little golden rope, the blue curtain fell away to reveal four columns of names etched into a plaque. Eve noticed the name *Valentina Holmes* at the top of the first column – Max's mum. Rhi's parents were there too, and Ollie's. At least half the names on the plaque matched the names of local people and businesses that Eve had known her whole life.

"This will be hung at the retail centre when it opens in the summer," said her father, "so that every visitor will know and understand the generosity of the people of Heartside Bay. Without them, our project would never have got off the ground."

This brought the loudest round of applause so far. Eve had never realized how many of her friends' parents had invested in the development. It gave her a warm feeling to the tips of her toes.

Time for the next Josh phase, she decided.

She turned to him with her widest smile. "Let's get everything ready for this afternoon while the others take a tour of the office."

Josh scratched his ear. "Where are we going to be this afternoon anyway?"

Eve pushed him through a door towards the back of the office. Josh flung his hand up to his eyes, startled at the burst of brilliant sunlight that greeted them.

They were in a large glass room that extended off the back of the office block like the stern of a ship. The cliffs, the town and the sea were all visible through the huge floor-to-ceiling windows. In here, Eve always felt high above everything, like a seagull coasting on the wind without a care in the world.

"This is what I call a meeting room," said Josh, gazing round in amazement.

"It's Daddy's best conference room," Eve said proudly. "I've given him strict instructions not to show anyone else this room until later, when we do the activity I've designed. We have to make everything perfect."

Josh looked at the great glass table in the centre of the room, stacked neatly with paper, pencils and calculators. "Looks pretty perfect to me already."

"We're dividing into fourteen pairs," said Eve. She pointed. "The big table in the middle divides into lots of little tables. We'll line them up around the room. Make sure every table has the same number of pens, pencils, pads, calculators and water glasses."

"Mustn't forget the water glasses," said Josh.

Eve whacked him. Not too hard, but hard enough

to show that she meant business. "Don't tease me," she said. "Get to work."

The conference table was like a big glass jigsaw. With a bit of coaxing, Eve and Josh managed to separate it into its constituent parts, which they arranged in four rows. They counted out pens and pencils, moved chairs, and straightened pads of paper.

"All done," said Eve at last, standing back to admire their handiwork.

"Lila had it right," Josh said. "You really are something."

"I'm not sure Lila meant it as a compliment," Eve said with a little laugh.

"Well, I do," Josh said.

Eve examined her fingernails in a show of embarrassment. Peeking up through her eyelashes, she felt encouraged by the admiring look on Josh's face. Letting her triumph wash over her like a warm, scented bath, she put a gentle hand on Josh's sleeve.

"There's one more thing," she said, gazing up into his green eyes. "I've convinced Daddy's advertising department to use you to design the official logo and signage for the shopping centre!"

Josh's mouth dropped open. "You what?"

"You heard," said Eve, delighted by Josh's reaction. "Daddy loves the logo you designed for today. He wants to use you, Josh. He'll pay you and everything. Isn't that brilliant?"

A whole range of emotions chased each other across Josh's face: disbelief, pride, excitement.

"You. . ." He threw his arms round Eve, hugging her so hard that for a moment she feared for her ribs. "You are amazing. Thank you," he said into her neck. "A thousand times thank you."

"It was nothing," said Eve. She felt a little breathless.

Josh pulled back and looked at her. For a heartbeat, Eve stared at his lips. This was it. The kiss. She had been waiting for it. Longing for it. Hadn't she?

She felt herself stiffen and pull back. Josh released her at once.

"Is . . . everything OK?" he said, sounding a little startled.

Eve gazed at Josh's puzzled face in mortification. Why had she pulled away? What was wrong with her?

"Yes," she said awkwardly. "Everything's fine. It's all . . . fine."

He looked perplexed.

Eve wanted to grab herself by the shoulders and shake herself, hard. She had just wrecked the very moment she had been working towards. And she had no idea why.

FIVE

Got to push through the awkwardness, Eve thought. She'd done it before. She could do it again. Nothing was going to ruin today. Not even her own stupidity.

She applied one last coat of mascara, and smoothed her hair so that it sat sleekly on her shoulders. No one could tell she had just had one of the most embarrassing experiences in her life. She would smile at Josh and act like everything was fine. Easy.

"Wow, Eve, you look . . . focused," said Lila as Eve marched out of the bathroom, tucking her mascara into her bag.

"I'm always focused, Lila," said Eve. "Does everyone have a partner for this afternoon's task?"

Lila had paired up with Ollie. Rhi and Max had

drifted together, although Eve thought Rhi didn't look too pleased about it. Polly was with Ryan Jameson.

"Do I have to be with Ryan?" Polly said in a low voice to Eve. "Something tells me he'd prefer to be with Lila."

Ryan was gazing across the glass conference room at Lila with a lovesick expression on his face.

"Sorry, Polly," Eve said briskly. "Just do your best."

Mr Morrison started issuing instructions about behaviour around the town centre as Eve made her way across the room to join her own partner. She was determined not to blush.

"Planned our victory yet, Josh?"

"I was waiting for you," he said in surprise.

"Have you read the instructions?" Eve asked, despite knowing them by heart. She had, after all, designed this task specifically to her and Josh's strengths.

"'Come up with a product to sell at the Heartside Shopping Centre'," Josh read. "'You will need a product name and a print ad to advertise your product. Presentations in the boardroom at four o'clock.' I guess there isn't much we can do until we've done our research, right?"

10Y was already drifting out of the glass conference room in pairs, discussing their plans. Josh started forward to join them, but Eve held him back.

"We're not taking the lift with everyone else, silly," she said. "We'll take Daddy's special lift. He brings all kinds of important people into his office that way. People that don't want to be stared at by the whole office, you know?"

"That lift is reserved for Mr Somerstown's guests, Eve," Gloria said, starting up from her desk as Eve pressed the executive lift button.

"My whole class are Daddy's guests today, Gloria," said Eve, pushing Josh into the lift. "He won't mind."

The sun was out, and the weather was mild. Eve and Josh headed to a café to discuss some ideas.

"I was thinking maybe healthy snack bars," Eve began. "We can put something together for everyone to try in the boardroom this afternoon. I can't think of anywhere in Heartside Bay that sells— what *are* you doing?"

Josh was doodling a mad-eyed seagull on the pad

of paper between them on the café table. "Working on our product logo." He turned his sketch to face Eve. "What do you think?"

A seagull stood guard over a pile of nuts and dried fruit. In a graffiti-style font, Josh had scrawled GO NUTS over the seagull's head.

"Are you mad?" said Eve, giggling. "We're not selling bird food."

"Nuts and seeds *are* bird food," Josh pointed out, grinning.

Eve scrunched up her nose. "I was thinking of something a little more elegant than a greedy seagull."

Josh promptly drew three ladies sipping tea with the same logo over their heads. The absurdity of it made Eve laugh even more. *I don't laugh often enough*, she realized. *It felt good.*

They left the café with a list of the town's food shops to visit, in order to sound out the competition. Eve's gut feeling had been right – there were very few places where you could buy healthy snacks in the town. When she finally persuaded Josh to ditch *Go Nuts* in favour of the more elegant-sounding *Fruitful*, everything was in place for what Eve felt sure would be a task-winner.

"We just need to invent candy floss made of carrots and we'll be millionaires," Josh observed.

"I'm going to experiment with mixes," Eve decided. "We can offer the results to everyone in the boardroom to taste."

"I love how you keep things simple," Josh said, rolling his eyes.

"Just concentrate on the logo. I'll do the rest."

They carried a bag of ingredients back to the office, together with a few utensils and three shallow tins. As Eve mixed combinations of ingredients and pressed them into the tins to chill in the office fridge, Josh worked with Somerstown Developments' art department to produce their print ad: a graphic image of the word FRUITFUL in a colourful, blocky font.

"We are brilliant," said Eve happily, standing back to admire their table in the glass conference room. Everything – the cranberry-and-cashew-butter squares, the banana-and-date-syrup bars, the peanut-butter-choc-and-chilli swirls and the FRUITFUL ad – looked amazing.

Now they had the product displayed so nicely, the pitch was easy to put together. When they finished, Eve checked her watch. "It's only three o'clock," she said, surprised. "We're even better at this than I thought."

Josh tried a peanut-butter-choc-and-chilli swirl, flapped his hand in front of his mouth and nodded in agreement at the same time. "Where's everyone else?" he said around a mouthful of swirl.

"Who knows," said Eve, slapping his hand away and covering the snack bars in a layer of cling film. "They'd better hurry up if they want to get something together for the judges at four."

"Let's go and see if we can find them," Josh suggested. "We could help them if they're struggling. We've got plenty of time left."

Helping the competition wasn't part of the plan. "I'm sure they're fine," Eve said dismissively.

Josh raised his eyebrows at her. "Don't be mean, Eve. And we'll take the normal-people lift this time. I don't want to be responsible for giving your dad's secretary a heart attack."

Feeling a little irritable, Eve let Josh drag her to the lifts and back into the town again. Her feet were starting to hurt, and she wasn't in the mood for bailing out any of her idiot friends. If they couldn't hold it together for a simple business task like this one, they didn't deserve her help.

They passed most of the pairs heading back to the Somerstown Developments offices, chattering through print-ad plans with their arms full of sample products. Max and Rhi however weren't carrying anything at all.

"Tech support," said Max when Josh questioned them on their product. He thumbed himself in the chest. "The product is me."

Eve felt irritated. Max Holmes had come up with Max Holmes? Typical.

"So where have you been all this time?" she accused.

"Sitting in the Heartbeat Café watching Tech Man put away three bowls of ice cream," Rhi groaned. "Come *on*, Max, you've left me hardly any time to design the print ad."

Eve and Josh heard Lila and Ollie before they saw them. They were squabbling like the gulls screaming over the bay.

"I can't *believe* you didn't ask them."

"*You* were supposed to be asking them!"

"Don't you have ears, Ollie? I told you—"

"You told me, blah blah blah. Maybe I don't like being told, Lila. Has that ever occurred—"

It made a refreshing change, seeing Lila and Ollie at each other's throats. *Not such a perfect couple after all*, Eve thought.

Realizing they had an audience, Lila and Ollie stopped yelling at each other and regarded Eve and Josh warily. Ollie's face was red with anger. It wasn't a good look, Eve decided.

"We can't wait to see what you two are going to show us in the boardroom," she drawled. "Squabblers United: we'll have all your arguments for you!"

Lila looked like she was almost in tears. "Shut up, Eve."

"Is there anything we can do?" Josh asked.

Lila shot another poisonous look at Ollie. "Do you do assassinations?"

"What are we going to do?" Ollie said fretfully. "There's no time left."

Eve sighed. Did she have to do all the thinking around here?

She nodded at an accessories shop across the road. "Go in there and get a handful of necklaces or something. You'll have to wing the rest. It's almost four o'clock and I don't want to be late for the presentations. Come on, Josh."

Grabbing Josh's arm, she towed him back towards her dad's offices. They had a task to win.

Mr Morrison was chatting to two members of her dad's management team and – surprisingly – the principal of Heartside High, Mr Cartwright. What was he doing here? Eve glanced around for her dad. She checked her watch. Ten to four.

The big room was a riot of colour and conversation as people hung posters and arranged products on their tables in preparation for their presentations. Eve started feeling nervous.

"I've made a special detour to be here this afternoon on request," called Mr Cartwright over 10Y's heads. "And I don't have much time. Shall we get started?"

"Mr Cartwright shouldn't be on the judging panel," said Eve fretfully. "It should be Daddy."

"Your father was called away about half an hour ago," said Gloria, passing Eve with a sheaf of paper in her arms. "Urgent business. Your principal has kindly stepped in."

Eve felt her eyes pricking with tears of disappointment. Her dad was supposed to be judging this, and seeing how brilliantly she had done everything. He was then supposed to round off her away day with one of his special speeches that would make everyone laugh. But he had left her all by herself.

Josh nudged her. "Are you OK?"

Eve was relieved she'd had the foresight to wear waterproof mascara. "Of course I'm OK. Now are we winning this thing or what?" she snapped.

The presentations weren't as much fun as Eve had hoped they would be. Everything had taken on the greyish tinge of disappointment. She smiled blindly for the room as she went through the pitch, letting Josh offer their healthy snack bars to the judges. The other teams presented a blur of accessories, beauty treatments and wash-off tattoos that made no impression on Eve at all. She didn't even have the energy to enjoy Ollie and Lila stuttering their way through a presentation about stacking bangles that they'd called – in a brief moment of inspiration – Off the Cuff. When she and Josh were called out as winners, she felt nothing at all, except the papery crinkle of a thousand pounds' worth of shopping vouchers for the future shopping centre pressed into her hand by Mr Cartwright.

"Thank you everyone for coming," she said mechanically as the applause died down. "It's been a great day for Heartside High and Somerstown Developments."

"A thousand pounds!" Polly said in awe as Eve joined Josh and the others munching through what was left of the Fruitful products. "I've never even seen a thousand pounds before."

"It's not real," Lila said. "It's just vouchers. And the shopping centre's not even finished yet anyway."

"Looks real enough to me," Max said, eyeing the wad of paper in Eve's hand.

"What do you want to do with it?" Josh asked Eve enthusiastically.

Eve couldn't muster any enthusiasm for the last part of her plan. She summoned a smile from somewhere.

"You take half, Josh," she said. "You guys can take the rest."

"Oh my God, Eve, seriously?" Lila gasped. "You're giving each of us a hundred pounds?"

"Real now, isn't it Lila?" said Ollie, taking two

fifty-pound vouchers and slipping them into his pocket.

Lila's eyes narrowed. "Back off, Ollie."

Rhi and Polly squealed and hugged Eve in delight, almost crushing her between them.

"You're the best, Eve!" said Rhi.

"I'll fix your computer any time you like," Max said, rubbing his two fifties between his fingers. "For free."

Eve had known the money would bring her friends back to her side. She felt a strange swell of resentment. *It's not just boys who are predictable*, she thought sourly. *It's girls too.*

Suddenly there was the sound of a smash. Somerstown Developments staff and Heartside High kids alike instantly fell silent at the drama unfolding beside the main lifts.

"That is IT, Ollie Wright," Lila screamed as Ollie stared in shock at the bangles Lila had thrown on the floor. "You and me are *over*."

"Fine by me, you bossy cow," Ollie shouted back angrily.

It looked as if Heartside High's golden couple had just broken up.

SIX

Polly ran towards Lila. Max had shoved Ollie backwards and was talking to him, low and fast. The shopping vouchers lay forgotten on the table as the rest of 10Y whispered with excitement and Mr Morrison and Mr Cartwright tried in vain to bring some kind of order.

Eve had been wanting to see Ollie and Lila break up for so long that it took several moments to process that, finally, it had happened for real. A rush of annoyance broke over her. Of all the times to drop this particular bombshell, Lila and Ollie had to do it on her away day? Now the break-up would be all anyone talked about back at school, and Eve's hard work would be forgotten.

Typical. It made Eve want to scream.

Lila pushed Polly away and ran down the stairs, tears streaking her cheeks. Without a backward glance at Eve, Josh hurtled after Lila. Eve was bleakly amused to see him push Ryan out of the way at the top of the stairs.

So much for Josh and me, she thought despondently.

Eve watched as Max patted Ollie on the shoulder and then left, taking the lift down with Rhi. A fantastic thought suddenly struck Eve and all at once, her spirits rose.

Something good might come out of this after all, she thought.

She marched up to the sullen-looking Ollie and took his arm.

"Come with me."

Ollie looked startled, but followed Eve obediently back through the office to the executive lift.

"Not again," tutted Gloria.

"Last time Gloria. Today, anyway." Eve was suddenly feeling so cheerful she blew the old secretary a kiss as the lift doors closed.

Ollie looked distractedly around the plush interior

as the lift descended. Watching him, Eve folded her arms and leaned against the mirrored back wall of the lift.

"That was bad," she remarked.

Ollie grunted.

"I know just what you need," Eve said in her most soothing voice.

"I doubt it."

Eve wagged a finger at him. "Don't give me a hard time, Ollie. I'm *helping* you. This lift takes us straight to a private door into a side street. We can avoid the gawkers."

Ollie thawed a little. "Thanks," he said. "That would be . . . you know. Good."

Eve had planned this day down to the last detail. This final little treat had been intended for her and Josh, to clinch their romantic deal. But seeing how she'd already messed that one up, Ollie was the next best thing.

I mean the *best thing*, she reminded herself a little gleefully. Finally, maybe this was her chance with Ollie. At last, she could have him to herself. Show him what a good pair they made. By the time she'd finished with Ollie, Lila would be a distant memory.

She checked her reflection in the lift mirrors, and was pleased with what she saw. The sparkle was back in her eyes.

"Where are we going anyway?" said Ollie as they came out of the lift into the shady side street.

"The harbour," Eve said, flashing him a sideways smile. "We're going for a little sail on Daddy's yacht."

The thunderclouds on Ollie's brow lifted. "We are?"

Eve ran through the wardrobe she'd taken to the yacht the night before. She had chosen a selection of her favourite clothes to really wow Josh. Something told her that Ollie would like them too.

"I was going to use the yacht this afternoon anyway, so the crew is expecting me," she said casually. "I want to throw a party on one of the islands off the harbour, but I can't decide which one." She smiled. "Maybe you can help me decide."

Ollie's handsome face flushed with excitement. "Seriously? I'd love that. Heading for an island sounds *awesome*." He glanced over his shoulder at the town, his expression darkening briefly. "The further away from Lila I can get, the better."

Eve couldn't help smiling to herself. She dipped her

head so her hair fell flirtatiously over one eye. "Feeling more cheerful now?"

There was a clear spring in Ollie's step as he took the gangway in three quick strides, gazing up at the tall masts and smooth shining deck of the Somerstowns' yacht. The crew appeared from nowhere with two glasses of cold orange juice.

"First-class treatment," Ollie said with pleasure, swirling his juice around the tall crystal glass.

"Daddy always has the best," Eve said proudly. "Make yourself comfortable. The crew knows where we're going. I'm just going to change."

The yacht slipped its moorings and sailed out into the harbour. Eve quickly changed into her favourite white jeans and striped jumper, with her new red sandals from Paris. A grey cashmere scarf around her neck and little gold studs in her ears and she felt a million dollars.

She found Ollie gazing off the prow of the yacht, the wind blowing his thick blond hair into peaks. He looked sad.

"Are you OK?" Eve asked.

Ollie shrugged. "Not great," he said honestly.

"Give yourself time," Eve said, laying her hand on his sleeve.

"Lila and I were over a long time ago," Ollie confessed with a sigh. "We both want different things, you know? I just wasn't brave enough to make the break." He looked even sadder. "And I've had this feeling for a while now that she likes someone else anyway."

I bet she wants to get her claws into Josh, Eve thought. How neat and perfect that would be. It would probably all work out really nicely for Lila. She was one of those girls who always came up smelling of roses.

"You're better off without her," she said fiercely.

"I guess." Ollie flushed and fiddled with his glass. "And if I'm honest, I've kind of . . . liked someone else for a while too."

Eve felt a little thrill in the pit of her stomach. Had Ollie preferred her to Lila all along?

"And . . . do you think this person likes you too?" she asked, feeling a little breathless.

"I feel really bad even talking about this," he said with a sheepish laugh. "I mean, Lila and I only broke up about ten minutes ago! But . . . I think she might. What should I do?"

I mustn't rush this, Eve thought exultantly. "The heart knows what it wants," she said, and she squeezed Ollie's arm lightly.

Ollie's smile lit up his handsome face. "You're right. You're always right, Eve, aren't you?"

Eve imagined Ollie's face cradled in her hands. His lips pressed against hers. "I don't know about that," she said lightly. "But I do my best."

The islands were coming into view. Eve leaned on Ollie's shoulder and pointed at one of the smaller ones, a green triangle with high cliffs at the back and a wide sandy shoreline. "That's the one I want for the party," she said into his ear. "Shall we check it out?"

Ollie was like an excited schoolboy as the yacht moored at the little jetty that jutted out from the island. He rushed ashore with a whoop.

"This is awesome!" he gasped. "I've always wanted to visit one of these islands, and now here we are! We have the whole place to ourselves! A party here would be incredible, Eve. How many people are you going to invite?"

60

"About fifty." Eve pointed at a patch of level, grassy ground, feeling excited as she imagined how everything would look. "I thought we could have the marquee there, and flares all along the shore. The dance floor will be on the beach, and we'll have a fire pit and live music and a Caribbean theme."

Ollie looked like he couldn't believe his ears. "It's going to be *beyond* incredible if you do all that."

Eve bathed in the warmth of Ollie's admiration. She checked over the island one more time. Yes, she thought. It would do very nicely.

As the sun began to dip below the clouds, they headed back to Heartside Bay. The air was cool, but not unbearable, so Eve and Ollie stayed up on deck watching the waves.

"I really needed this," said Ollie, gazing towards the pinprick lights of Heartside Bay's harbour. "My head is feeling so much clearer. Thanks for dragging me along."

He surprised Eve with a hug. Eve wrapped her arms around Ollie's back and returned the pressure, nestling her head against his neck.

"Ollie?" she said into his shirt.

"Hmm?"

"How come we never got together?"

Ollie stiffened. "I don't know," he said.

Eve snuggled a bit closer. They fitted together so well. "We would have made the perfect couple," she said softly.

The orange glow of the sky was all around them.

"I guess the timing was never right," Ollie said slowly.

They pulled apart and stared at each other.

"And now would be completely the wrong time, of course," Eve said, gazing at him. "You only just broke up with Lila."

"Yes." Ollie's eyes were wide, fixed on Eve's mouth. His arms tightened round her. "Now would be a really . . . bad . . . time. . ."

Eve opened her mouth at the pressure of Ollie's lips. She pulled him close, feeling his short blond hair between her fingers. It felt triumphant and exciting, to be kissing Ollie. The only thing missing was Lila to witness her victory.

Some part of Eve detached itself. Suddenly she felt as if she was watching herself on a screen. She kissed

Ollie a bit harder, trying to enjoy the kiss. Where was the spark? If she couldn't find it with Ollie the school heart throb – the boy of her dreams – then how was she ever going to find it? It was so disappointing, she could cry.

Ollie pulled back.

"Sorry," he said sheepishly. "Got a bit carried away there, didn't we?"

Eve felt the tears rising. "Don't worry about it," she said as casually as she could manage.

Ollie stared at the deck. "Right," he said at last, glancing awkwardly at her. "Well, like I said. Thanks for everything."

Everything except the kiss, Eve thought, feeling bleak.

The yacht bumped gently against its moorings in the harbour. Ollie held out his hand. "See you," he said.

Eve shook Ollie's hand, every part of her dying with humiliation. "Sure," she said, smiling bravely. "See you."

SEVEN

Eve didn't know how she got through the rest of the week. Her usual confidence was a little tattered at the edges. Lila and Ollie were avoiding both her and each other. Josh had caught Eve's eye a couple of times on Thursday, but hurried away before Eve could talk to him. Eve wondered bitterly if he had kissed Lila yet.

Her cheeks burned with humiliation every time she thought about her kiss with Ollie. The way Ollie had pulled back. That horrible, awkward goodbye. She wasn't bad at kissing. Neither was Ollie. So why hadn't it worked? Eve shuddered. The memory wouldn't leave her alone.

The only way out of the misery was to find a

fresh focus, Eve decided. It was time to get her party underway.

She threw herself wholeheartedly into the planning. Straight after school on Thursday, she headed for her favourite stationery shop and selected some beautiful thick invitation cards in a bright Caribbean blue.

I'll print them in gold, she decided, *and put them into matching envelopes filled with sparkling sand.*

Feeling happier now that she had one decision under her belt, she hurried home to draw up a list of guests. Wriggling out of her school uniform, she threw her clothes haphazardly into the laundry bin and took a long, hot shower. Then she snuggled into her favourite cashmere pyjamas and hopped into her big white quilted bed, threw on some reggae music to get her in the mood, and started to draw up her ultimate guest list. There would have to be a mix, she decided. Not just kids from school, but other friends as well. *Everyone* in Heartside Bay would know about Eve Somerstown's latest incredible party. She'd be the talk of the town.

Eve spent Friday in a pleasant daze, compiling playlists of the perfect music and imagining the best way to serve drinks and nibbles on a beach. They would use banana leaves as plates. Eco-friendly and imaginative. Her mouth watered at the thought of the gorgeous Caribbean food she would serve to her guests. The only problem she could foresee was the tiny matter of pinning down a suitable boy to take.

Why did boys have to ruin everything?

When the bell rang for the end of class on Friday, Eve remained at her desk, staring at her extensive to-do list. She had chosen three weeks on Saturday as the date for her party. It would be a rush to get everything done, but she liked it that way. It gave her less time to think about other stuff.

Her phone buzzed in her pocket. She tugged it out.

Hi Evie. Come to the office after school?
Dad xx

Eve hadn't seen much of her dad since the away day; it had felt as if he was permanently in meetings, or travelling. She hadn't even had a chance to ask him what he had thought of all the hard work she'd done to make the away day a success. It was frustrating, given that she'd done it all for him to begin with.

I hope nothing's wrong, she thought, pocketing her phone and breaking into a gentle jog towards the doors. *Daddy's been acting so stressed lately.*

Eve reached Somerstown Developments a little out of breath, and took the normal lift to the top floor. The office was busy as usual. Eve gave everyone a brief glance, checking for stressed faces, bad news. Everyone seemed calm, even cheerful. But Eve still felt anxious.

"Daddy wanted to see me, Gloria," she told her father's secretary without preamble.

Gloria rustled through a pile of papers by her telephone. "Did he now? Well, I'm afraid you've missed him."

Eve was in no mood for this. "That's ridiculous," she snapped. "He told me *specifically* to come to the office after school. Why wouldn't he be here to meet me?"

Gloria nodded behind Eve. "I believe he wanted you to meet Caitlin."

Eve swung round.

"Hello," said the beautiful dark-haired girl behind

her. She smiled, revealing a set of perfect white teeth. "You must be Eve."

Eve felt flustered. "Where's Dad?" she blurted. "Who are you?"

"Manners," muttered Gloria behind her desk.

Caitlin's glossy ebony hair framed her smooth, heart-shaped face set with large, warm chocolate-brown eyes. She looked a little older than Eve, maybe eighteen or so. "Don't worry Gloria," she said, giving the old secretary a dazzling smile. "There's obviously been a bit of a miscommunication. Eve, I'm Caitlin Matthews. Your father arranged for me to come over this afternoon and meet you."

Mechanically Eve shook the pale hand extended in her direction. She had no idea what was going on. Her cheeks felt hot.

"I run a party-planning business," Caitlin continued. "Your dad thought we could have a useful conversation. You're planning something on one of the islands off the coast, right?"

Eve was completely thrown by this strange girl's presence in her father's office. For the first time in her life, she didn't know what to do. "Um," she said at last, "yes. A party."

Caitlin's eyes gleamed. "Fantastic idea for a venue," she said. "I've never organized anything on an island before."

Eve tried to get a grip on the conversation. "My dad asked you to help me plan my party?"

Caitlin nodded. "Our fathers are in business together. Well," she amended, flashing another heart stopping smile, "they aren't in business yet, but this afternoon's meeting should fix that. My dad is hoping to invest in Somerstown Developments."

At last, something was starting to make sense. "And while they talk business, Daddy thought you could help me plan my party?" said Eve.

Caitlin laughed. "Exactly. If you don't mind a little help?"

Part of Eve felt a little outraged that her father thought she needed help. The rest of her felt excited. "I'd like that," she said, feeling strangely shy. "I'm hoping to hold the party three weeks from tomorrow, and there's loads to do. I've made a start, but you know what it's like."

"Three weeks?" Caitlin whistled. "We have *oceans*

of time, don't you worry about that. I bet you've already been making lists." She linked arms with Eve and grinned at her. "I can tell this one is going to be *fun*."

There was a warmth about Caitlin that made Eve feel more relaxed than she had in ages. "Great," she said happily. "So . . . do you want to discuss it now?"

"There's no time like the present," Caitlin said. "Do you mind if I have one of these, Gloria?"

She picked a mint from the bowl that always sat beside Gloria's computer and waved it enquiringly at the secretary. Eve held her breath. She'd never dared help herself to Gloria's sweets.

"Have as many as you like, dear," said Gloria cheerfully. "They don't do my figure any good."

"You have a *fabulous* figure, Gloria," said Caitlin, wagging a beautifully manicured finger at the secretary. "Never let anyone tell you otherwise."

Eve marvelled at the way Caitlin had so effortlessly made the grumpy old secretary smile. She felt a rush of admiration for her unexpected new friend.

"Come on, Eve Somerstown," said Caitlin through the mint wedged in her cheek. "Let's go and find somewhere cosy to make plans."

"Take the executive lift if you like, dear," said Gloria unexpectedly. "It's the quickest way out of the building."

"Fantastic!" Caitlin clapped her hands with delight. "I've always wanted a ride in an executive lift. Gloria, you are a *darling*."

Eve tried not to stare at Caitlin's reflection in the lift mirrors as they descended to street level. She was flawless from every angle. Her clothes, her hair, her skin. It was like she had a light glowing inside her. She made Eve feel dull, childlike. The school uniform didn't help.

Down at street level, Caitlin waved her keys haphazardly in various directions until a gleaming red soft-top car started blinking some way up the street.

"I can never remember where I've parked," she said, striding towards the car.

Caitlin's car was almost as gorgeous as Caitlin.

"Where are we going?" Eve asked, sliding into the passenger seat.

Caitlin patted Eve on the leg, making her jump. "To a great little place I know. Believe me, it's guaranteed to get us in a party mood."

Eve fiddled with her shirt collar. "Caitlin?" she said. "Do you mind if we stop at my house first? I really want to get out of my school clothes."

"But that little blazer is adorable," said Caitlin in surprise. "So chic."

"I'd really like to change," Eve said, laughing.

"Whatever you say."

The little car roared away from the kerb with a squeal. Eve leaned her head against the headrest, feeling the cool air buffeting her face.

She felt suddenly alive with – something. Hope, maybe.

EIGHT

Feeling a lot more comfortable in a pair of jeans, a light-green V-neck, and a soft white cardigan from Paris, Eve relaxed as Caitlin urged the little red car along the coast, away from the town. The houses grew fewer and further between as the road switched and snaked up and down, through hills and down to the sea and back up again. She wondered curiously where they were going. Surprisingly, she found that she didn't care.

Caitlin was chattering at full speed about the last party she had organized. "Chic" was her favourite word.

"Everything was *unbelievably* chic. We put long silver birch twigs inside a dozen tall glass vases, filled the vases with water and put floating candles on the top. The whole place *glowed*. Such a good idea. I impress even myself sometimes."

"How long have you had your party-planning business?" Eve asked.

"About eight months now," said Caitlin, changing gear smoothly. "I have a storeroom filled with the most delectable things imaginable. Decorations, candles, crockery."

"Balloons?"

"I *adore* balloons," said Caitlin happily. "Have you read that Sylvia Plath poem about balloons? Oval soul animals, she calls them. Have you ever seen the glittery helium ones with lights inside? They look amazing gathered in bunches on the ceiling. So much of a party atmosphere comes down to good lighting."

She took a sharp left, the car wheels crunching over gravel. Eve sat up curiously. Caitlin seemed to be heading towards the cliffs themselves. The only thing up there that Eve could think of was a spooky old abandoned lighthouse.

The lighthouse loomed over the brink of the hill. It was even taller and more forbidding up close than it was from a distance. Eve felt the first flush of unease as Caitlin brought the little car smartly to a halt and jumped out.

"Come on!" Caitlin said, laughing.

Eve gazed at the selection of expensive cars parked carelessly on the grass around them. She got out of the car very slowly and looked at the lighthouse with apprehension. The crumbling brickwork was stained with salt and lichen. It wasn't the kind of place to put *anyone* in a party mood.

Caitlin was already at the weather-beaten red door. Eve hung back as she lifted her hand and rapped smartly on the salt-stained wood.

The door opened a crack. A well-dressed man with a heavily crooked nose frowned through the gap. "Yes?"

He looks like a boxer, thought Eve. A well-dressed boxer, but a boxer nonetheless. What was going on?

"Don't make that scary face at me, Ali," said Caitlin. "I know you're expecting us. Be a darling and let us in before the wind blows us off the cliff."

A broad smile lit the scary man's face. "In you come, Caitlin my love. You and your friend look frozen stiff."

Walking through the lighthouse door, Eve had a confused impression of warm, flickering light. A log fire glowed in the centre of the rounded room, smoke issuing up a long central chimney. A low, comfortable hum of conversation assailed her, together with the most delicious smell of herbs and coffee.

A few people looked up as she and Caitlin entered. Eve felt the shock of sudden recognition at the sight of two well-known local footballers relaxing by the fire with an expensive-looking chess set laid out between them.

"I hope you're letting Leo win, Carlos darling," said Caitlin, dropping two kisses on the bigger, more famous footballer's stubbly cheeks. "You know how bad-tempered he gets about losing."

"You tell him, Caitlin," grunted Leo Mullins, tugging a little irritably on his goatee as he stared at the board. "He won't listen to me."

"It does him good," said Carlos, draping a friendly arm around Caitlin's slim waist. "Who's your friend?"

"Eve," said Caitlin, beckoning Eve over, "I want you to meet the cleverest men in football, Carlos

Andrade and Leo Mullins. They also throw the best parties, although that's mainly down to me."

Eve was struggling to stay cool. Not much surprised her, but this . . . was unexpected.

"Pleased to meet you," she managed, holding out her hand.

"So English," said Carlos giving her two loud cheek kisses. "We are more friendly in Portugal. Are you in the party business too?"

Eve shook her head, feeling a little overwhelmed at being so close to someone so famous. She was so glad she'd changed her clothes. "Caitlin's helping me organize one."

"Whatever the girl says, do it," said Leo. "She's a party genius." He knocked over his king with a sigh. "You win Carlos, you old goat."

"Dinner is on you, Leo," Carlos crowed, and Leo grumbled and laughed and pulled a shiny black credit card from his back pocket to pay for dinner.

Eve recognized at least two other people in the room with the fireplace – a film actor and a guy who presented property shows on TV. She felt Caitlin's warm hand in hers, pulling her on through the room.

"Carlos and Leo are both darlings," she said, giggling. "And they pay very well, as you can imagine."

"What *is* this place?" Eve said. "Why have I never been here before?"

She prided herself on knowing all the best places in Heartside Bay. She wasn't the queen of the teen social scene for nothing. But this was like no place she'd ever seen.

"It doesn't have a name," said Caitlin cheerfully. "It doesn't need one. Members-only, of course. Terribly exclusive. And you have to be recommended by three members and approved by the entire membership. You have to be eighteen to join. That's probably why you haven't heard of it yet. Dad got me in. Fun, isn't it?"

A large room that appeared to be made half of glass was the next surprise. Eve felt a little dizzy at the sight of the sea crashing away almost beneath her feet. The light was astonishing, pale and full of the sea, washing through the vast salt-speckled windows and over the elegant guests. There was more of the same low hum of conversation in here, people chatting over delicate slices of cake and tall frothy glasses of coffee, the occasional sound of loud laughter ringing overhead.

They took a small twisting flight of stairs painted bright red and hung with signed photographs of all the rich and famous club members to the next level: a warm modern space hung with valuable-looking paintings. People sat quietly at tables here, hunched over laptops. Others chatted at the bar, teetering on designer heels.

"Oh, you *must* meet Hermione," said Caitlin suddenly. "Hermione, this is my friend Eve. I'm planning a party for her."

Eve found herself folded into the heavily perfumed embrace of a world-famous rock star's ex-wife.

"Caitlin organized such a wonderful event for us this summer," said Hermione, in a husky voice. "The girl is gold dust. Have some fun for me."

"Now *that* was a party," reminisced Caitlin, towing the almost-speechless Eve onwards. "A rock star in every cupboard, a black and white Pierrot theme. Hermione wanted to fill the swimming pool with champagne, but I persuaded her that sparkling water would be far more chic." She giggled. "Less sticky too. We did a champagne fountain instead. We had underwater lights that changed colour," she added dreamily. "The effect against the bubbles was *heavenly*."

Eve had always thought her parties were the best parties in the world. But it sounded like Caitlin had taken parties to a whole new level. She was only a couple of years older than Eve, but it was clear that she was brilliant at her job. Eve felt almost faint with excitement at the thought of what she and Caitlin might create between them.

"Let's sit somewhere and start planning," she begged, catching Caitlin's arm.

"In the party mood, are we?" Caitlin teased.

"Totally!" Eve fumbled in her bag for the special jotter she'd brought to write down ideas. "Where can we sit?"

Caitlin pushed her gently onwards, towards the next flight of stairs. "I've booked us a room," she said, her eyes twinkling. "Right at the top."

Eve's brain was awash with ideas, each one more outrageous than the last. She and Caitlin together, Daddy's usual limitless budget. This was going to be *legendary*.

The view from the top of the lighthouse was breathtaking. Eve's legs ached from the long climb up the dizzying stairs, but it was worth every twinge. She could see for miles through the plate-glass windows that provided an unrivalled 360-degree view of Heartside, the ocean and the hills inland. Eve pressed her hands to the glass and watched the clouds scudding in from the sea, changing shape as they moved. Sea mist started rippling up the coast, washing back and forth like smoke. The roofs and spires of Heartside sat below them like a toy town.

A table had been laid with a white cloth and a large vase of scented white roses. Caitlin poured fresh lemonade into a glass and pressed it into Eve's hand, smiling into her eyes.

"Do you like the view?"

Eve nodded wordlessly.

"Let's order some food," Caitlin suggested. "I'm starving. We can plan as we eat."

They sat at the little white table, enjoying the view and the chilled lemonade, swapping stories about their lives. They had so many people in common, Eve was amazed they had never met before.

The sun started setting, spreading red-gold fingers of light across the white tablecloth between them. Between mouthfuls of crispy, piping-hot calamari dipped in silky yellow mayonnaise and a wildly colourful salad, Eve couldn't write down her party ideas fast enough. A live steel band to deliver the invitations. Coconut-shell candles on barrel-shaped tables. A thatched beach bar, fire-eaters, sand sculptures. Caitlin listened and advised, topped up their glasses and told stories about all the astonishing parties she'd helped to organize.

"But this is going to be the best one yet," she smiled, clinking glasses with Eve. "I can feel it."

The whole evening had been so perfect that Eve felt a little dazed.

She couldn't think of anyone she would rather have spent the evening with.

NINE

"Are you on your phone *again*?"

Eve finished tapping out her latest text to Caitlin and pressed send before looking absently at Rhi. "What did you say?"

Rhi folded her arms. "Keep your phone out of sight, Eve," she said. "Even you won't be able to get it back if a teacher sees you texting in class."

Rhi had a point. The teachers at Heartside High were serious about confiscating phones. Eve checked Mr Morrison's whereabouts very carefully before looking at her screen again.

Caitlin had replied already.

**Dyed doves are gorgeous idea darling but
not sure they live in the Caribbean?
#dyeaparrottoday
Cxx**

Eve snorted. Rhi looked at her in surprise.

"What?" said Eve, recovering.

"If I didn't know you better, I'd say you were laughing," Rhi observed.

"I laugh," Eve objected, feeling put out. Her fingers itched to type a funny reply to Caitlin. "It's just that my humour is a little more sophisticated than most people in this dump."

"Sorry I spoke," said Rhi with a shrug, turning to Lila on her other side.

Parrots, thought Eve. Why hadn't she thought of parrots before? Parrots would be incredible. She could have five – no, *ten* parrots flying around the party. All different colours. She could picture them now, squawking and soaring on gorgeous wings over her beachside dance floor.

Let's do parrots!!!

Exx

Using a live steel band to distribute the party invitations was my best idea ever, she thought happily as she pressed send.

Caitlin had organized everything perfectly. The whole school had turned out on Monday morning to gawp as the three-piece band strode down the corridor playing on their drums. She'd had a tricky conversation with Mr Cartwright after, but it had been so worth it. *Everyone* was talking about her party, just as Caitlin had promised.

Lowering her phone, Eve caught a few smiles aimed in her direction.

They're only smiling because they like the way you spend your money, whispered a treacherous little voice in her head.

Her good mood dipped a little.

Buzz.

Know just the person to squawk to. #parrots

Cxx

Thank goodness for Caitlin, Eve thought gratefully, tucking her phone away where Mr Morrison wouldn't see it. It was lonely being rich. Caitlin understood that so well. Caitlin understood her so well.

The bell rang for the end of the lesson.

"Can't wait for the party, Eve."

"I've been practising limbo dancing, Eve!"

"Can I bring my brother to your party?"

"Can I bring my best friend to your party?"

"Oh Eve, Eve, can I bring my cat to your party?" said Josh in her ear as Eve pushed through the crowd attempting to corner her by the classroom door.

"Get me out of here, Josh," Eve said. "Can we go to the beach?"

She was glad Josh had returned to his normal friendly self after their weird almost-kiss last week. It had been a surprisingly long week without him.

The beach was empty as usual, and especially windy. Eve pulled her hair back into a ponytail, then sat on the beach wall and kicked her legs idly against the stones. Josh had already taken out his sketchbook and was drawing the curling, crashing waves.

"Are you coming, then?" Eve asked.

Josh leaned a little closer to his sketch. "Coming to what?"

Eve rolled her eyes. "My party, of course?"

"You've invited me, haven't you?" Josh said. "Everyone knows you don't turn down an invitation from Eve Somerstown."

"Don't tease me," said Eve. "Are you really coming?"

Buzz.

Orchids or hibiscus for the leis?

Cxx

"Do you think we should have orchids or hibiscus for the leis?" Eve asked Josh.

Josh sighed. "I have no idea what you're talking about."

"You know, *leis*. Fresh flower necklaces? It's more Hawaii than Caribbean, I know, but Caitlin thinks it will add a lovely touch."

"I'd go for plastic ones myself," said Josh.

Eve grimaced. "I don't do plastic. I think . . . orchids."

She typed the reply and pressed send. Caitlin responded with another question almost immediately.

Waiters in grass skirts. Too much?

Cxx

"Do you think the waiters should wear grass skirts, Josh?" Eve asked.

Josh looked up from his sketch for a third time. "Eve, these questions are better suited to someone who isn't trying to draw in peace," he said with obvious irritation. "Don't you think?"

"I don't have anyone else to ask," Eve pouted.

Josh put his sketchbook down and regarded her. "Of course you do! There's Rhi, Polly, Lila—"

"*Lila?*" said Eve in disbelief. "Lila hates me, Josh. And believe me – it's totally mutual."

Josh shook his head. "You're your own worst enemy, Eve. Lila's lovely. The most genuine girl in the whole school."

"Fancy her, do you?" said Eve waspishly, and had the brief pleasure of seeing Josh blush.

"I hate all this drama with you girls," he muttered. "It's so stupid."

"Josh, *I'm* not the drama queen here," said Eve, swelling with indignation. "It wasn't me who broke up with her boyfriend in the middle of an away day so everyone would talk about that instead of the brilliant business day they'd all experienced. You're only saying this because you want to go out with her."

"I don't!" Josh stuttered. "We're just friends!"

Eve snorted disbelievingly.

"OK then, what about Rhi?" Josh asked. "You've been friends for years."

"She hates me even more than Lila does," Eve muttered. She did miss Rhi.

"And whose fault is that?"

"Max Holmes," Eve said sulkily. "It takes two people to kiss each other, you know."

The air turned sticky. Eve knew with painful certainty that both she and Josh were thinking of their near kiss in the glass conference room.

"Anyway, Max and I were over ages ago," she said, keen to move things on. "And he and Rhi look like they're getting back together."

"Fine," said Josh. "So talk to her. Now, if you'll excuse me, I'm going to find a six-lane motorway where I can do my sketching. It will be a lot quieter than this beach."

Eve drew moodily in the sand with her toe as Josh

closed his sketchbook and headed away from the sea without her. Boys didn't understand a *thing*.

The thought of a dreary classroom full of girls who hated her filled Eve with dread. She decided to blow off the rest of the afternoon and find Caitlin. She deserved a bit of time with someone who liked her.

You free now?
Exx

No I'm horribly expensive. But open to suggestions.
Cxx

Eve could feel herself relaxing already. She dialled her dad's office.

"Gloria? Can you call the school and let them know I'll be gone for the rest of the afternoon?"

She texted Caitlin next.

Pick me up at the Grand Hotel in 10?
Exx

"Where are we going?" Caitlin said, peering over the top of her aviators as Eve slid into the passenger seat of her little red car. Caitlin was wearing an expensive pair of black leather trousers and looked like she belonged in a magazine.

"Somewhere that isn't Heartside Bay."

Caitlin nodded in understanding. "Via yours to change?"

Within twenty minutes, they were purring towards the motorway. *Towards freedom*, thought Eve, adjusting her Ray-Bans and wriggling her toes luxuriously in her red Paris sandals. She always felt more alive when she was with Caitlin.

"You're very quiet," Caitlin remarked. "Everything OK?"

"You know when everyone hates you?" Eve remarked, trying to keep her voice light. "That."

"Who could hate you?" Caitlin said in surprise. "You're about to give the party of the *century*."

"You'd be surprised," Eve said drily. "I've messed up a lot of things in my life lately, and I don't know how to unmess them. Does that make sense?"

"Tell me," said Caitlin.

Eve began to talk. She took Caitlin back to the day Lila had first turned up at Heartside High and upset Eve's world. How Lila had stolen Ollie from Eve; how Eve had stolen Max from Rhi. How horrible it had felt, being unpopular. And how much she found herself hating the way everyone was sucking up to her again now that her party was on the horizon.

"I mean, I planned it this way," Eve groaned. "The whole *point* of the party was to make everyone like me again. And I've got that. At least, kind of. So why am I still feeling so miserable? So . . . lost?"

"Girlfriends," said Caitlin.

Eve felt a little startled. "What?"

"Everyone needs girlfriends," Caitlin said. "Mates to talk to. Friends to pick you up when you're down. Kick you in the tush when you misbehave."

"You're that person," said Eve, blushing a little.

Caitlin waved her down. "I'm one person, darling. You need your gang back. Someone as beautiful and talented as you should never make enemies."

Eve's heart felt strangely full. "That's the nicest thing anyone's ever said to me."

"Then you need to get out more," said Caitlin

kindly. "Friends are important, Eve. Romance comes and goes, but friends should be forever."

Eve nodded. As always, Caitlin made perfect sense. "You're right. I've been stupid, letting boys get between me and my friends, haven't I?"

Caitlin laughed.

"So what should I do?" Eve asked. "How can I get my friends back?"

"Darling," said Caitlin, changing gear, "you have come to the right person. Don't you know by now that I have all the answers?"

TEN

"But who is it *from*?" Rhi repeated, staring at the printed cream invitation.

"How would I know?" Lila said, gazing at her own invitation.

Polly took Rhi and Lila's invitations and compared them. "Same as mine," she said in disappointment. "No name. No clue. Just . . . this."

"Relax and enjoy a free night with us at Heartwell Manor," Rhi read. "Dinner and breakfast included."

"I went to Heartwell Manor once," said Polly. "For a party. I didn't stay, though."

Listening at her locker two doors down, Eve didn't miss the way Polly shuddered. She winced at the memory of kissing Polly's old boyfriend in the

94

Heartwell Manor gardens. Another reason for her friends to hate her.

"Maybe you won it," she said, looking over as casually as she could.

"All three of us?" Rhi scoffed. She frowned at the looped gold writing on the heavy card. "I never win anything."

"Me neither," said Lila, sliding the card into her locker. "It's probably a scam."

Eve bit her lip. She could do without Lila casting doubt on the sender's motive. Already Rhi and Polly were frowning.

"When is it?" she asked.

"Tonight," said Polly, studying her invitation more intently as if it would suddenly give up its secrets.

"Did you get one of these?" Lila asked, looking directly at Eve.

Eve shook her head. On that, at least, she was being entirely honest. "You must have entered a competition or something," she said, filling her bag with the right books for the morning's classes. "Clicked 'Like' on Facebook without reading the small print. We've all done it."

"Oh!" said Rhi, her eyes opening a little wider. "I did click on something recently."

"Me too," said Polly. "That must be it!"

Lila took her invitation out of her locker again and reread it. "Maybe," she said, sounding doubtful.

Just one more push, Eve thought.

"If you go," she said, "you have to try the lobster. It's incredibly expensive, but worth every morsel."

"Dinner is included," Lila said. She cocked her head thoughtfully. "It doesn't say anything about not including extremely expensive lobster. I've never had lobster."

"There's a pool and a spa," Polly said, biting her lip. "One bad experience shouldn't put me off Heartwell Manor, should it? I never even stayed the night. Their beds are supposed to be the softest in the world."

Eve could tell her friends were wavering.

"You only live once," she said, putting her bag over her shoulder. "Go and see what it's like. You might never get another opportunity."

Turning her back on her friends, she headed down the corridor and into the darkening afternoon. If this didn't work, she thought ruefully, she was in for a lonely night.

Heartside Manor was looking particularly lovely in the clear evening light. Eve sat tensely by the fireside in a big blue wing chair, sipping her juice and checking her watch. She'd arranged everything for her friends in connecting suites at the top of the hotel, with views over the gardens. Gifts, food. Everything except the truth. That this was her attempt at apologizing, and getting her girlfriends to like her again.

She heard Lila's voice first, echoing through the tiled foyer beyond the bar. Eve's heart leaped. She knew no one entering the hotel could see the person sitting in this particular chair if they curled their legs up and kept very, very still. She did exactly that.

"Hello, can I help you?"

Eve heard the sound of the invitation being plonked on to the reception desk. "Um, yes, I hope so," Lila said. "We got these invitations today."

"We don't know who they're from," said a second voice.

"We think maybe it's a competition?" said a third voice.

Eve closed her eyes gratefully. Lila, Polly and Rhi had all come. This was going well – so far.

"Of course," said the receptionist smoothly. "We are expecting you Miss Murray, Miss Nelson, Miss Wills."

Eve heard Polly's explosion of giggles. She snuggled a little deeper into the wing chair, listening.

"We'll take your bags up right away," the receptionist continued. "Here are your keys. Have a pleasant stay with us at Heartwell."

"This isn't a key," Eve heard Rhi say in surprise as her friends passed the high back of her chair. "It's a credit card."

"It's a key card," said Lila. "Haven't you ever seen one before? I am so having lobster tonight."

Eve waited until the elevator door slid shut with an expensive purr. Then she uncurled her legs, tried to calm her loudly beating heart, picked up the carrier bags she had stowed by her feet and took the elevator to the third floor.

Suites 304 and 305 were the best rooms in the hotel. Eve's dad was always recommending them to visiting business associates. Eve herself had once spent a

Christmas Eve in Suite 305, watching TV and bickering with Chloe while their parents dined downstairs.

She paused outside Suite 304, her key card in her hand. It was stupid, feeling this nervous. Eve straightened her back.

"Room service," she said bravely, opening the door and stepping into the pale pink carpeted room.

Rhi, Lila and Polly stared at her, open-mouthed. Polly had already put on her hotel bathrobe.

"What are you doing here, Eve?" said Polly at last. The ties on her robe trailed on the soft pink carpet behind her.

"I'm your host, of course," Eve said, doing her best to sound light-hearted as she moved into the centre of the spacious room. "Isn't this lovely?" She swung the carrier bags hopefully at her friends. "Goodies for everyone."

"This is *your* sleepover?" said Rhi, looking confused. "What about the competition?"

"There was no competition," said Lila scornfully, putting her hands on her hips. "I knew this was too good to be true. Come on, guys. Let's go."

Eve felt panicky as her friends headed for the door.

"No, wait. Wait! I . . . wanted to apologize to you. To all of you. I . . . I . . ."

Friends to kick you in the tush when you misbehave. She could hear Caitlin in her head, as clear as a bell. This was her last chance to fix things.

"I've been a total idiot and a bad friend and I'm sorry," she said in a rush. "Please stay. There's an explanation!"

Lila marched back towards Eve. "An *explanation*? What is there to explain? You've made all our lives miserable. You tried to steal our boyfriends. I think that's enough *explanation*."

Tears welled up in Eve's eyes. "I've been a bitch. I know I have," she said in a small voice. "You don't know how difficult it is, being me."

Lila laughed in amazement. "Now I've heard it all!"

"Quiet, Lila," said Rhi. She sat down on one of the wide white beds. "Let's give Eve a few moments."

Hot tears ran down Eve's cheeks. She let them fall. It was a strange feeling, letting herself be vulnerable like this. "One minute everything was great," she sniffed. "Then Lila came along."

Lila glared. "I've heard enough of this."

Eve caught Lila's arm as the dark-haired girl headed towards the door again. "I'm just saying what I felt! I'm not saying I was *right* to feel that way, OK?" She looked hopelessly at the hostile faces of the three girls around her. "I'm sorry Rhi, for the whole Max business. I'm sorry Polly for the way I treated you." She swallowed. "And I'm sorry for not making you welcome when you came to Heartside Bay, Lila. I was . . . jealous, I think."

Eve was surprised to hear herself say it out loud. Jealous. She'd been jealous, all along.

"Jealous?" echoed Lila incredulously. "Of me?"

"Don't kid yourself, Lila," Eve said with a waspish flash of her usual self. "You're beautiful. And popular. You'd only been in the school for five minutes before all the boys started falling for you. You took Ollie."

"For all the good it did me," said Lila sourly.

There was a long silence.

"Listen, Eve *has* apologized," said Rhi at last. "We should give it a go."

Polly shrugged, clearly trying to keep the peace. She waved her arms around the room at the warm blankets folded on the ends of the beds, the basket of hot chocolate and biscuits on the dressing table, the widescreen TV and the huge marble bathroom. "We do have all this to try before the night is out."

Lila grunted, but sat down on the end of a bed.

"Good!" Eve said, relieved. "Time for presents."

She gave everyone a swish little carrier bag. "PJs," she said nervously. "Designer, naturally. I think I got the right sizes." She hoped the others actually liked what she'd bought them. "I've got us all face masks too. Lovely organic ones. Mummy uses them every week. You wouldn't believe how. . ."

. . .*expensive they are*, she was going to say. Something in Lila's face stopped her. "How nice they are," she finished a little lamely.

Everyone took their presents silently out of the bags and looked at them.

Eve rushed on.

"Room service! We can order the lobster if you like. I know Lila wants to try it. I'll just order us some lemonade first. They make it with real lemons here – it's gorgeous. Does everyone like lemonade?"

Rhi put her PJs gently down on the bed. "Eve, stop trying so hard," she said.

Eve rubbed her temples. Her hands were trembling. "Sorry." *How many times can one person say sorry in an evening?* she wondered a little hopelessly.

"I want to have a massive bubble bath," said Polly, disappearing into the bathroom. A moment later there was a squeal. "There are TWO bathtubs in here! OMG, and I think they're Jacuzzis!"

Lila's eyes brightened. "Let's get our swimming costumes on. Everyone brought them for the spa, right? We can share the tubs."

"All of us?" said Rhi in surprise.

Polly put her head round the bathroom door. "They're big enough for four people in each," she said, giggling. "Come on!"

Everyone started taking off their clothes and rummaging through their bags for swimming costumes. When a startled-looking room-service waiter appeared at the door with two large jugs of chilled lemonade five minutes later, a half-dressed Rhi shrieked and ducked behind the bed.

"Oh man," Lila sighed, relaxing at last into the steaming bubbles of the Jacuzzi she was sharing with Rhi. "That poor guy's face."

"What about *my* face?" Rhi objected. "I've never turned so red in my life!"

Everyone roared with laughter. Eve dipped her head back into the bubbles, feeling the water massaging her head. She felt all her nerves and anxieties about the evening swirling away, light as the scented bath foam they were using. Everything was going to be all right.

"Thanks for doing this, Eve," said Polly as Eve came up again for air.

"Any time," Eve smiled.

They made the Jacuzzi last as long as they could, before Rhi started complaining of wrinkly fingers. Then, dressed in their cosy new PJs with their Heartwell Manor dressing gowns over the top, the girls sat down in a comfortable circle on the floor to have the most delicious room-service lobster picnic in the world.

The face packs were next, followed by assorted bottles of nail polish for some experimental manicures. Rhi found some decent music on a radio station and Polly made hot chocolate for everyone to drink.

"Not bad, Eve," said Lila, lolling back against the

bed to admire her black and white yin-yang nails. "Not bad at all."

There was a knock on the door. Eve padded over to see who it was.

"Caitlin!" she shrieked in delight.

Caitlin was swathed in an expensive-looking shearling jacket, dark trousers and heeled ankle boots. "Hi babes," she smiled, peering over Eve's shoulder into the room. "I just thought I'd come by and see how you were getting on."

Eve hugged her impulsively. "It's turned into the most brilliant evening. Come and meet everyone. Everyone, this is Caitlin. Caitlin, this is Lila, Rhi and Polly."

"I feel a bit underdressed," said Lila, looking down at her PJs.

"Given the choice," said Caitlin, throwing down her shearling on the bed, "I would wear PJs *all* day. A silk polka-dot pair. So chic. What are we doing?"

"Oh, can you stay?" said Eve in delight. Could this evening get any better?

"We're about to play truth or dare," Polly giggled. "Do you want to join us?"

"Oh darlings, I'd shock you terribly," said Caitlin with a careless shrug.

"We're not that easy to shock," said Lila, rising to the challenge.

Caitlin settled down on the floor between Eve and Lila. "Fine," she said with a glint in her eye. "Truth."

"Have you ever stolen anything?" Lila asked, grinning.

Caitlin thought. "I stole a Lamborghini once, for about five minutes," she said. "I almost drove it into the swimming pool."

"No!" Lila gasped. "Seriously?"

"It was at a party," Caitlin giggled. "I would have taken the Rolls-Royce, only I couldn't reach the pedals."

"Your turn, Lila," Rhi said. "Truth or dare?"

"Truth," said Lila.

"Would you take Ollie back if he asked you?"

"I wouldn't touch Ollie again if you paid me," Lila said at once. "I'm through with boys. They are so much *trouble*."

"I know what you mean," Rhi agreed with feeling.

"Girl power all the way!" laughed Polly.

"From now on," Lila declared, "I'm going to have fun."

"You haven't done one yet, Eve," said Rhi. "Truth or dare?"

Eve decided she'd bared her soul enough for one night. "Dare," she said, feeling a little flicker of nerves.

"Kiss Caitlin," Lila giggled.

The others gasped.

"I'm game if Eve is," said Caitlin with a laugh.

It's just a game, Eve reminded herself. And she pressed her lips to Caitlin's.

ELEVEN

The strangest feelings coursed through Eve as she felt Caitlin's lips moving against hers. Instinctively she opened her mouth, and felt a little electric shock at the feeling of Caitlin's tongue.

She broke away, dimly aware of cheering.

"I can't *believe* you just did that, Eve," Rhi gasped, giggling madly.

"She loved every second, look at her," Lila joked. "I've never seen you blush before, Eve."

Eve was feeling breathless. Confused. She couldn't look at Caitlin. "If that's the hardest dare you can think of, you're losing your touch, Lila," she said, trying to make light of it.

She could feel Caitlin looking at her. *Don't look*

back, she thought. She was scared of what she might see.

A loud hammering on the door made everyone jump out of their skins.

"Strippergram," shouted a familiar voice.

Rhi covered her face. "It's Max!" she gasped.

"And it sounds like he's brought half of 10Y with him," sighed Lila at the sound of laughter on the other side of the door.

"How did they know we were here?" asked Polly.

"I got their details from the list for the party and invited them," Caitlin said, getting up. "I hope it's not a problem? The best parties have a mix of girls *and* boys, in my experience."

Eve took the opportunity to move to the far side of the room. She wanted to put as much distance between herself and Caitlin as possible. What had just happened?

It was just a game, she told herself. *Don't think too hard about it.*

"About time you lot opened up," said Max, striding into the room with Ollie, Ryan and Josh. He looked around admiringly. "Nice place. Can we stay too?"

Lila and Ollie looked warily at each other. Ollie made his best puppy-dog eyes, and Lila laughed reluctantly. "OK," she said, rolling her eyes. "Since you're here you might as well stay. But no funny business."

"Not even with me?" smirked Ryan.

Lila ignored him, tugging on Josh's arm to bring him further into the room. Eve winced on Ryan's behalf. His attempts at flirting with Lila always fell flat.

"Do you want to talk?"

Caitlin had somehow sneaked up on Eve and was now standing beside her, hands in her pockets and head cocked to the side.

"What about?" said Eve, sidling away. "There's nothing to talk about."

Caitlin's brown eyes were serious. "Sure?"

Eve's laughter sounded brittle to her own ears. "This is a party," she said awkwardly. "We have guests to see to. Right! Who wants lemonade?"

She threw herself into a whirlwind of what she was best at: looking after party guests. Soon everyone had a glass in their hand, sandwiches had been ordered on room service and Max was squirting Ollie with some scented hand lotion he'd found in the bathroom. Ryan hung around the edges in his usual way, slouching on and off the balcony and sighing.

Somehow amid the laughter and sandwiches, Caitlin had slipped away. Eve sank into the comfortable chair at one end of the room and rubbed her eyes. She didn't want to think about the kiss, but she couldn't help it. Even the memory sent a shiver through her.

"This is boring," Ryan complained from the balcony. "Let's go out."

Lila looked up from where she'd been laughing on one of the beds with Josh. "Have some more crisps, Ryan. This is *fun*."

"Well I'm bored," Ryan repeated sourly. "We should all head into town. Do something crazy."

Ollie made jazz hands in the air, making Polly laugh. "Like what? Frappés at the Heartbeat? Everything's free here, Ryan, hadn't you noticed?"

Hardly free, Eve thought before she could stop herself. She shook her head impatiently. What was wrong with her? Everything had been going so well, her friends were having a great time – and she just felt ratty and irritable.

"I was thinking about somewhere better than the Heartbeat," said Ryan casually.

"Where?" Max said, looking interested.

"The shopping centre."

Everyone went quiet. Lila's eyes gleamed.

"That place is only half-built," Ollie said at last. "We're hardly going to get access, are we?"

"Isn't that the point?" Ryan drawled.

"That's trespassing, mate," said Max.

Eve thought Ryan looked bigger, somehow. As if by getting everyone's attention, he'd grown two inches.

"So?" he said, strutting from side to side. "I'm man enough. The question is – are you?"

"Up to the challenge, boys?" Lila drawled. "Because I am."

Ryan puffed out his chest a little more. "I knew Lila would see it my way. Who's in?"

Eve felt the old familiar flick of jealousy. Lila only had to click her fingers and boys came running. She wondered what her dad would make of them all climbing around his shopping centre in the middle of the night.

A little kick of rebellion fluttered in her stomach. The thought of having the almost-complete shopping centre to themselves. . . It would be a like a giant playground. And it would take her mind off Caitlin, that was for sure.

"I am," she said out loud. Just because she was a Somerstown, it didn't mean she couldn't play every now and again.

"Fine," Max said, rolling his eyes.

"I don't know," said Polly, looking worried.

"Come on," said Ollie, putting his arm round Polly and giving her an encouraging squeeze. "It'll be fun."

It didn't take long to convince the last remaining doubters. The girls ran into the bathroom to change out of PJs and back into jeans and sneakers. They all tiptoed out of the suite, squeezed into the lift and headed into the cold night air.

It was a short walk downhill to the construction site. Its huge glass and steel walls loomed over them, the cranes silent, the diggers parked haphazardly to one side. A single night security guard patrolled aimlessly past the main entrance, flicking his torch from side to side briefly before disappearing.

"Now's our chance," Ryan said.

"Last one's a chicken," Lila giggled.

Eve could feel her bravado deserting her. This had felt like it might be fun, back in their suite at the hotel. Now she wasn't so sure. Construction sites were dangerous places.

Ryan had reached the main entrance already. Lila wasn't far behind him.

"Losing your nerve?" Ryan taunted the others.

"Shut up, will you?" Max hissed. "Do you want the security guy to come back?"

Thinking about the cosy hotel suite had brought Eve's thoughts back to Caitlin. Desperate for distraction, she turned to Josh. Maybe she could fancy him again. How hard could it be?

"I'm scared," she said, slipping her hand through the crook of Josh's arm. "You won't leave me alone in this place, will you Josh?"

Josh fiddled with his glasses. "I'm not traditional hero material," he observed. "Ollie and Max are the knights in shining armour around here." He nodded at the two boys, who had already jogged over the road to join Ryan. Lila, Rhi and Polly followed, their nervous laughter echoing in the darkness.

"You could always draw a knight if I needed one," Eve said, fluttering her lashes. "You're so talented, it would probably leap off the page and charge us all down."

Josh looked flattered. "Let's catch up with the others before they leave us behind."

They ran quickly through the entrance and into the vast central space with the others – and stopped, looking around in awe. Two partially complete flights of stairs ascended from the ground floor to the top, where the restaurants would be. Silent escalators cut silver zigzags up and down the open space from floor to floor. Dangling wires and scaffolding poles gleamed in the moonlight filtering through the high glass roof. The winking red lights of the cranes could be seen far overhead.

"This is even better than I'd hoped." Ryan jogged over to one of the half-completed staircases and tested it with his weight. "Race you to the top!"

"Ryan, I don't think it's safe," said Rhi uneasily.

"Come on Rhi," Lila scoffed. "I thought we'd talked about having some fun for a change!"

But Ryan was already halfway up, leaping over the

gaps like a monkey climbing up a tree. He sat on the edge of the open-sided mezzanine floor, dangling his legs over the edge.

"Come on," he shouted down, laughing. "It's no fun alone. I don't know what you see in these losers, Lila."

Lila folded her arms. "No one likes a show-off, Ryan."

"That's not showing off," Ryan grinned, getting to his feet again. He pushed his hair out of his eyes. "*This* is showing off."

Rhi and Polly both gasped as Ryan heaved himself on to a piece of scaffolding and swung there for a moment, bringing his feet right out over the open space below.

"I'll join you," Max said, clearly not happy at being upstaged. "The stairs don't look that difficult."

"Apart from the huge hole halfway up, through which you might plunge to your death?" enquired Josh a little sarcastically.

"Yeah," Max said with a casual shrug. "Apart from that."

Eve was wishing they hadn't come. There was a

wildness about Ryan in here that made her nervous. The weight of responsibility on her shoulders was unpleasant. This was her father's place. What if something happened?

Ryan was now climbing to the next mezzanine floor, two levels up. "I bet you can't get this high!" he shouted down at Max, grinning.

"Ryan, stop!" Polly implored. "Don't go so far!"

Eve felt a little ill.

How far *was* Ryan prepared to go?

TWELVE

"Let's play hide and seek," Ollie suggested.

Ryan was back on the ground, doing press-ups in the middle of the great marble floor with Polly and Lila giggling and cheering him on.

"Ryan's such an attention-seeker," said Rhi. "Why did he even come with us?"

"Don't be too hard on him, babe," Max said easily. "He just wanted a good time. And we're having a good time, aren't we?"

"We do still appear to have all our limbs in working order," Josh said. "That has to be a good thing."

"Hide and seek?" Ollie repeated, rubbing his hands. "There are some awesome hiding places in here. Who's seeking?"

Josh seemed the keenest to keep his feet on the ground, so Josh was first seeker. Eve darted away into the darkness with Rhi. This *was* pretty fun. She had been worrying about nothing.

"Are you serious?" she said in horror as Rhi squirmed underneath a freshly cast concrete bench near the back of the shopping centre. "You'll get filthy!"

"Shhh!" Rhi whispered. "Run Eve, before Josh sees you."

Eve ran on, her breath clouding in the chilly air. Spotting a curve in the wall, she swerved out of sight and pressed herself up against the bare concrete.

"Sixty-eight and a half, coming ready or not," shouted Josh.

Eve heard Ollie's voice echoing as if from very far away. "You're supposed to count to a hundred!"

"Lovely clue as to your whereabouts, Ollie!" Josh shouted back. "Thanks for that."

Several laughs echoed around the complex, including Eve's. Ollie could be a real idiot sometimes.

Leaning back against the cold concrete, Eve gazed up at the great glass roof overhead. It reflected the whole complex back at her. It was going to be fantastic when it was finished.

Not long now, she thought, hugging the thought close. Her dad had said it would only be a matter of weeks before the first businesses moved in.

"Behold the invisible woman."

Eve jumped to see Josh peering at her round the corner. "How did you find me?"

Josh pointed up at the glass roof. "It reflected your red coat beautifully. Guess you're the next seeker."

"OK, so you got me," Eve said.

She sat on Rhi's concrete bench. She almost screamed when Rhi grabbed her ankle.

"That's a funny face," said Josh in surprise.

"The bench is cold," Eve explained, fighting to keep a straight face. She looked around the space. "How are your plans for the shopping centre logo coming on?"

"I have lots of ideas," he said eagerly. His face fell a little. "But your dad's too busy to discuss them at the moment, so I have no idea whether I'm on the right track or not."

"He won't forget about you," said Eve. "I promise." She hoped that was true. She hadn't really spoken to her dad for days. Not properly. She vowed to herself that she would remind him of his deal with Josh as soon as she could.

Josh prowled twice around the complex before spotting Rhi underneath Eve's bench. Ryan was hiding on the second mezzanine floor. Josh refused to climb up to get him, so he was declared the winner of round one.

"Round two: no climbing," said Max irritably. Josh had found him lurking near the entrance shortly after finding Ollie lying underneath an escalator.

"Come on, you did win the first game," said Lila as Ryan rolled his eyes in an exaggerated manner.

"Fine," Ryan grinned. "As long as you hide with me this time, Lila."

"Your turn to seek, Eve," said Rhi breathlessly. There was a long smudge of grime down her trouser leg from hiding under the bench.

Eve covered her eyes to count. Visions of the kiss swam across her eyelids. The softness of Caitlin's mouth. The smell of her hair. She opened her eyes again abruptly, to catch a glimpse of Max scurrying for a pile of enormous concrete blocks stacked beside one wall. She frowned. She didn't know much about construction, but blocks that size weren't usually "finishing touches," as her father had described things in his speech at her business away day.

After a while, she realized she hadn't been counting.

"Coming," she shouted. "Ready or not!"

She loitered for a while before heading for the concrete blocks and pretending to be surprised to find Max and Rhi.

"Can we go home after this round?" Rhi asked as Max dragged her grumpily to sit with him on the bench.

Eve did a careful sweep of the right-hand side of the complex next. Shop after shop lay empty and bare, wires swinging from plasterboard ceilings. The words "finishing touches" came into her mind again. Being inside her own head was no fun tonight.

She swung round a corner, into one of the covered radial corridors that fanned out from the central space, past a stack of paint pots, a folded ladder and a battered tarpaulin – and almost crashed into two people wrapped tightly in each other's arms.

Ollie and Polly leaped apart.

"Er . . . you found us!" said Ollie brightly as Polly's cheeks deepened to a rich poppy red. "Well done!"

"Were you kissing?" asked Eve in astonishment.

"No," said Ollie.

"Definitely not," Polly squeaked, turning even redder.

Facts started whirring and clicking through Eve's brain. Cogs spun and settled. Ollie on the yacht. *I've kind of . . . liked someone else for a while.*

It was so obvious, now Eve came to think of it. These two had been weird around each other for ages. *Something else I was wrong about*, Eve thought to herself with a sigh. Ollie hadn't been talking about her on the yacht. He'd been talking about Polly.

Polly covered her burning face with her hands. "I got scared in the dark," she mumbled through her fingers. "And Ollie . . . Ollie just gave me a hug. Don't say anything!"

"Don't tell Lila," said Ollie awkwardly.

Eve raised her eyebrows even higher.

"I mean, Polly's right," Ollie amended, putting his arm round Polly's shoulders, "nothing actually happened other than a hug like she said, but . . . I don't want Lila getting the wrong idea. You know. So soon after we broke up."

"You won't tell her," repeated Polly, her voice high with anxiety. "Will you?"

Eve didn't like the way Ollie and Polly were looking at her. Like they were scared of her, and what she might do with this little bombshell. The old Eve would have tucked the information away, then dropped it into a conversation at a later date for maximum impact. *This* Eve – the Eve who had apologized to her friends, the Eve who had kissed a girl tonight and felt the old ground beneath her designer-clad feet shift and quiver – *this* Eve didn't have any interest in being mean. Seeing the two of them, the feelings they had for each other written clear as day on their horrified faces, just made her heart ache. Everything seemed so simple for other people.

"I won't say anything if you don't want me to," she said with a shrug. "Sit in the middle while I find the others."

They scurried away gratefully. Eve shivered, pulling her coat a little more tightly around herself. Why was it so cold?

Focusing on the radial corridor she was standing in, she suddenly realized why. The whole back wall of this section of the complex was open to the elements. Mud and rubble lay beyond the yawning space. Puddles of stagnant water glinted around muddy tools that looked like no one had touched them in weeks. Eve remembered the concrete blocks Max and Rhi had been hiding behind.

The complex was nowhere near finished, she realized, looking around. This whole section was a mass of scaffolding, plastic sheeting and mud. Uncertainty gripped her. *Finishing touches.*

Suddenly Eve's throat felt dry. She pictured the plaque with all the investors' names on it. Her father's smooth promises. The empty hulk she was standing in.

Had her dad been lying to her?

She shook her head. Her father was honest, hard-working . . . he would never lie about something like this. Would he?

There was a sudden clatter. An unearthly wail ripped through the air, echoing like a ghost against the exposed bricks.

"Help me! Someone, help! HELP!"

THIRTEEN

Eve spun round in shock.

"Help, I'm going to fall!" Lila screamed again. "I'm GOING TO FALL!"

Unfreezing her pose, Eve ran round the corner and back into the huge central space. Ollie and Polly were gaping upwards, their mouths open in fear. Max and Rhi sat frozen together on the bench. Following their terrified gazes, Eve stared upwards. The undersides of Lila's white trainers gleamed at her in the moonlight.

"I CAN'T HOLD ON!" Lila shrieked.

She was dangling from the first storey, swinging wildly, as Ryan tried to hold on to her, his face as white as bone. A splintered ladder lay at a useless angle on the ground floor beneath them both.

Eve saw in a flash what had happened. Ryan must have climbed to the first floor, using the ladder ... Lila had followed ... and at the last moment, the badly anchored ladder had slipped away, breaking as it crashed on the floor. Why had they gone up a ladder when there were stairs?

"Help me!" Lila moaned.

"Call the police!" shouted Ollie in horror. "Lila, hold on. . ."

He lunged for the steps. Josh was quicker, emerging from somewhere, leaping over the gaps in the stairway. There was a squealing sound as Ryan's trainers slipped on the bare concrete above them all. Lila lurched and screamed again.

"I can't hold her," Ryan moaned. "I'm trying. . ."

Josh was beneath Lila now, running frantically to and fro in search of something, anything to enable him to climb upwards. "Call the police!" he bellowed. "Call an ambulance!"

"We said no climbing!" Max shouted in horror. Rhi had buried her face in his shirt. "NO CLIMBING, RYAN! What have you done?"

Eve felt half dead with the horror of it. This was her

fault. She shouldn't have agreed to come here. Why was this place still so dangerous? So *unbuilt*?

Lila screamed again, hopelessly. It came out as a kind of croak.

"There's another ladder," Eve said, coming to life, remembering. "I'll fetch it. Hold on, Lila!"

And then she was running back to the corridor where she'd found Ollie and Polly in each other's arms, and lifting the ladder from among its tangle of tarpaulin and paint pots, and running through the half-built hallways with it, awkward and bulky in her arms.

"Nearly there, Eve!" Josh shouted.

"I'm going to die," Lila wept.

Don't trip, Eve thought as she clambered and slipped over the uneven floor. She felt the ladder gash a hole in the shoulder of her down jacket. Feathers drifted around her like smoke. The ladder felt heavy, so heavy. . . And then Josh was there, his hands grabbing at the metal struts, unfolding it until the top of it reached the edge of the first floor balcony.

A strange calm had descended on Eve. She knew what to do now.

"Lila, Ryan, I want you to listen to me," she said,

looking up. "Are you listening to me?"

"I'm going to die," Lila whispered.

"I can't hold her," Ryan moaned.

"There is a ladder," Eve said, speaking as clearly as she could. "Josh is holding a ladder just to the left of you."

"Yes," Lila gasped between sobs. "Yes . . . I see it. . ."

She stretched her toes – and made contact.

"Careful!" Rhi moaned, way down below.

Lila was shaking so badly she could hardly move. She hung where she was, one toe on a step of the ladder, her hands still holding Ryan's.

"Both feet," said Eve, steady and soothing. "Now a hand. Can you move a hand to the top of the ladder?"

"I'm letting go, Lila," said Ryan. He sounded calmer now. "You'll be fine now. I'm counting to three, OK? One, two. . ."

Lila made a desperate grab for the ladder. Eve found herself on the ladder now, climbing up towards Lila's shaking legs. "I'm here, Lila," she said. "It's OK."

"Three," Ryan finished, and let go.

Lila hugged the ladder with both hands now, weeping uncontrollably. Eve raised her hand, touched Lila's ankle. "One step at a time," she said. "I'm here."

Lila stepped clear of the bottom of the ladder as Josh folded her into a long, warm hug. Max, Rhi, Polly and Ollie cheered.

"Whoo!" said Ryan, lying on his back above them and laughing breathlessly. "What a ride! I thought we were both done for!"

Lila wept harder, clutching at Josh. Eve's cool deserted her completely.

"I wish you *had* fallen, Ryan," she hissed. "I wish you'd fallen and smashed every bone in your body! Lila nearly *died* because of you. Don't you get it? She doesn't like you! *None* of us like you! Don't you get it? You're pathetic."

Ryan had stopped laughing. Everyone was silent, holding their breath.

"You can forget about coming to my party," said Eve, shaking with all the fury and fright and confusion of her evening. "You can forget about ever hanging out with us again. We want you to leave. Now. Before someone else gets hurt."

Ryan climbed silently down the ladder, his face pale and set, his bravado gone. He touched Lila's shoulder.

"I'm sorry," he said.

"It's . . . my fault too," Lila gulped, wiping at her tears with shaking hands. "I shouldn't have climbed the ladder."

"Leave," said Eve in a voice of stone.

There was a burst of torchlight. Three security guards had appeared in the entrance of the complex, their beams sweeping the space. Eve shielded her eyes as a beam fell directly on her.

"Kids! Over there!"

"Run," said Max swiftly.

Everyone scattered. Josh dragged Eve and Lila over the half-built floor at rocket speed. Max and Rhi raced one way; Ollie and Polly raced another. Ryan had disappeared. There was the sound of boots clattering on the marble floor, muttered oaths and the jingling of keys.

"That way," Josh said in Eve's ear.

They bolted down the corridor where Eve had grabbed the ladder, leaping over the rubble, pushing through the tarpaulin. The shouts were getting closer. Eve crashed through a muddy puddle, feeling the chill oozing through her shoes. She fell, struggled upright again. She couldn't get caught.

"There's a gap in the fence over there," panted Eve.

"We'll never fit through that," Lila moaned.

Eve put on a fresh burst of speed, sploshing through the muck and trying not to think of her beautiful, ruined clothes. "We can do it," she said, and dived head first through the hole in the mesh.

She landed on a stretch of wet pavement, scraping her hand on the tarmac. Lila piled after her, followed by Josh.

"Keep running," Josh said, getting to his feet and doing his best to wipe the mud off his glasses.

Eve took off again like a hare, keeping pace with Lila and Josh not far behind. Part of her wanted to whoop and celebrate her freedom. The rest was still in the shopping centre, haunted by Lila's screams. A little way ahead she glimpsed Max and Rhi hurtling through the shadows, towards the beach and the sea.

Lila swung through a gate so fast Eve almost missed the turning. She stumbled over her own feet and landed in an ungainly heap on a stretch of wet grass, her breath loud in her ears. They had made it to the park. No one was following them any more.

They were safe.

FOURTEEN

Eve was finding it hard to concentrate on school on Monday. After the drama of the shopping centre, Lila's near-death experience and her own confusion about Caitlin, it was a miracle she made any notes at all during Mr Morrison's English class.

"If you're coming to my class," Mr Morrison said into Eve's ear, "it would be good if you could be present in mind as well as body, Miss Somerstown."

Eve jumped a mile in the air. Mr Morrison raised his eyebrows at the half-scribbled notes in her book and moved on.

Lila leaned across. "Everything OK?"

Everything's supposed *to be OK*, Eve thought in frustration. *But it's not.*

She knew she should be on top of the world. She'd had a wonderful sleepover with her friends, all of whom seemed to like her again, and her island party plans continued to blossom in exciting directions. But she couldn't focus on any of it. Instead, all she could see were the crumbling foundations of everything she had thought solid and real. Her father. Who she was, who she liked. . .

She summoned a smile for Lila. It was important to appear in control.

"Stop fussing, I'm fine," she said, rolling her eyes.

Lila looked dubious but didn't press it.

They made a crowd around the table at the canteen. Ollie and Max were full of the excitement of the shopping centre adventure, while Rhi and Polly wanted to change the subject and talk about the night at Heartwell Manor instead. Lila sat with Josh, making Eve wonder whether they'd got together at last.

That makes me the loneliest person on this table, she thought. *Rhi and Max. Ollie and Polly – if not yet, then soon. Lila and Josh likewise.*

"Everyone has their feet on the ground today, I see," Ryan tried to joke as he stopped by their table with his tray.

"No thanks to you," Eve said, looking up from the salad she had been prodding around her plate.

"Leave him alone, Eve," Lila said gently. "Ryan got as much of a shock as I did."

"Nothing scares me," said Ryan with a shrug.

"Then you won't mind sitting by yourself today," said Eve pointedly.

"Ha ha," said Ryan. "Joke. Right?"

The others moved up, letting Ryan settle himself next to Lila. Max clapped him on the shoulder. Sharing the weekend's drama seemed to have convinced everyone that Ryan was one of the crew now. It wasn't an opinion Eve shared.

After school, Eve decided she would go and visit her dad. She wanted to ask him about the shopping centre. Her finger hovered over her dad's number. After a moment, she put her phone away again. Now wasn't the right time, she realized. There was something she had to do first.

"Hey," said Rhi, passing with Lila and Polly. "Coming to the Heartbeat later?"

Eve shook her head. "Too much to do," she lied. "There's a problem with the caterers for the party, typical! See you tomorrow."

She waited until her friends had gone. Then she squared her shoulders and walked back the way she had just come.

The corridor outside Ms Andrews' classroom was quiet. Eve rapped at the door.

"Ms Andrews?"

The history teacher looked up from her computer. "Eve!" she said in surprise. "What brings you to my classroom this afternoon?"

Eve bit her lip. "Are you free?"

Ms Andrews nodded. She switched off her computer and perched on the edge of her desk. "How can I help?"

Eve remembered vividly the last time she'd spoken to Ms Andrews. When the scandal had broken about the history teacher being in a relationship with Polly's mother, Eve had found herself taking a special interest. She had worked hard to get Ms Andrews' job back when the school principal decided she should take a leave of absence. Ms Andrews had always been kind to Eve. Most importantly, she had listened when Eve had asked a question that had been troubling her for a while. Listened and not judged.

Ms Andrews, do you think it's normal to dream about kissing girls?

"Do you remember our last conversation?" Eve began a little nervously.

Ms Andrews nodded. "Of course. I was pleased you felt you could talk to me about it. Do you have another question?"

Eve sat down at a desk. "It's not a dream this time," she muttered. "I actually did kiss a girl. And . . . it was good."

There. She'd said it. She had liked the feeling of Caitlin's mouth on hers. The spark that she had been looking for in all the boys she had ever dated, the mythical electricity between two people that she had read about so often – it seemed that it was maybe real after all.

"Lucky you," said Ms Andrews. "I've had some awful kisses in my time."

Feeling a little shocked at her teacher's confession, Eve giggled.

"When you get a good one," Ms Andrews laughed back, "my advice would be to enjoy every moment!"

"But it wasn't *supposed* to be good," Eve blurted. She stopped, worried that she'd caused offence. "I'm sorry, I didn't mean—"

"I understand," Ms Andrews interrupted gently. "I was uncomfortable about it at your age too."

Eve couldn't imagine the self-possessed woman in front of her doubting herself for a moment. "When did you know?" she asked. "About . . . liking girls?"

"I think I always knew," said Ms Andrews. "But I pretended it wasn't true. I dated a few boys, but never very successfully. It wasn't until I went to university that I met my first girlfriend. She was called Clara. And suddenly . . . everything clicked into place."

"Were you with Clara for a long time?" Eve asked shyly.

"Not long," said Ms Andrews. She smiled. "But long enough to understand that I wasn't an alien from outer space."

Eve felt the tears wobbling behind her eyelids. She knew that feeling.

"Don't be afraid to be yourself," the teacher continued. "We only have one life. It's much too short to waste on worrying about what other people think."

Eve couldn't imagine ever *not* worrying about what other people thought.

She felt more scared than ever.

FIFTEEN

Eve waited, the phone pressed to her ear.

This is the voicemail of Henry Somerstown. Please leave—

She hung up, feeling lower than ever. Despite her best efforts, she hadn't managed to talk to her father all week. She'd almost managed a conversation that morning over breakfast, but a call had come through and her dad had left the house at speed, pausing only to pull on his cashmere overcoat and shout that he'd be out all day at a meeting in London. She'd tried him three times today, and reached voicemail each time. It was so *frustrating*.

"Heartbeat Café?" asked Rhi at the end of school.

"Not tonight," said Eve, pulling her coat from her locker. "Busy."

"What could possibly be more tempting than frappés at the Heartbeat?" said Lila on the other side. "Cocktails in Cannes? A film premiere in Leicester Square?"

Eve thought wistfully about sitting in the cosy café laughing with her friends.

"There's a big party happening on Saturday, in case you'd forgotten," she said out loud. "We only have a few days left and there is still so much to do."

"I thought that's what Caitlin was for," said Polly as she shouldered her bag.

Eve winced. She had been blocking Caitlin's calls for a couple of days now, limiting herself to answering Caitlin's questions by text. With the party only days away, the timing couldn't have been worse. But on top of everything else, she couldn't face a conversation with a girl she couldn't stop thinking about.

"It's still *my* party," she said coolly. "Whatever Caitlin's doing."

The house was quiet when Eve got in. There was always a kind of deadness at this time of day that she didn't like. Hanging her bag on a hook in the hallway, she took off her shoes and slid on her slippers. Her mother went mad if anyone ever tracked mud over the cream-coloured carpets. Then she went into the huge white kitchen and flipped on the radio. Music washed through speakers set into the walls, bringing a little life with it.

Eve opened the fridge, feeling hungry. Hummus, carrots and a lot of boring green vegetables stared back at her. Her mother had been on a health kick for a week now, and thrown out all the biscuits and juice in the house.

Crunching into a carrot, she wandered back across the wide hallway to her father's study. Locked, as usual. She took out her phone and tried him again, with the same result as before.

"Do turn that racket off, Eve, it's giving me a splitting headache."

Eve's mother had appeared in the door of the snug with a stick of celery in her hand, her highlighted blonde hair swept up on top of her head. She was swathed in white from head to foot like a designer snowman, with a soft white pashmina draped around her neck to hide the scars from her latest round of cosmetic surgery.

"OK, sorry." Eve returned to the kitchen and switched the radio off. "Where's Chloe?"

"Your sister has tap class on Wednesdays." Her mum paused. "Or is that Tuesdays? Perhaps it's riding today, I can never keep up. Yelitza's in charge of all that."

Eve often wondered how her mother would cope if the stolid home-help suddenly packed her bags and headed home to Venezuela.

"And 'OK' is such an irritating expression, I wish you wouldn't use it. So common and uninformative," her mother added fussily. "You're looking dreadfully tired, darling. That boxy black blazer does you no favours."

"I don't think they designed the Heartside High uniform with my skin tone in mind, Mother," said Eve, feeling a little stricken.

Her mum waved her celery stick at Eve like a conductor's baton. "Take the ghastly thing off. You know how affected I am by fabric. I feel like I'm having a conversation with a black widow spider."

Eve slid off her blazer and hung it up, glancing at her face in one of the hall mirrors.

Mummy's right, she thought fretfully. *I look awful.*

She'd do a face pack later. Maybe deep-condition her hair.

The thought of talking to her mother about problems was laughable. Tabitha Somerstown was only interested in success stories and perfection. A top grade at school? Tick. A main part in the school play? Tick. *Mum, I think I like girls, and what's going on at Dad's shopping centre?* was a lead balloon in the making.

Eve limited herself to a more practical question.

"What's for supper?"

"Heaven only knows," Eve's mother sighed, drifting away back into the snug. "I'm so dreadfully tired I can barely think, let alone cook."

Probably because that celery stick is the only thing you've eaten all day, Eve thought. She felt pretty tired herself. Munching on her carrot, she slowly climbed the stairs to her room, peeling off her hideous school uniform as she went, dreaming of the shower and her cashmere pyjamas.

Her homework took longer than normal. After three attempts, Eve decided it qualified as her best effort and pushed it aside. Her stomach was growling too loudly to be ignored.

Predictably, there wasn't much for supper. Eve poked at the remains of the gluten-free spinach lasagne Yelitza had made yesterday before taking herself back upstairs. All she had to do now was stay awake until her dad came home.

This is the voicemail of Henry Somerstown—

Eve stepped back on to the white-carpeted landing with her phone. "When's Daddy coming back?" she shouted down the stairs.

There was no answer. Eve guessed that her mother had gone to one of her gym classes. She went back to her room and lay on the bed for a while, staring at the ceiling.

When her phone rang, Eve snatched it up. "Dad?"

"It's Caitlin."

Eve froze.

"I just wanted to say that everything's been ordered, caterers are on standby, and I have the most heavenly outfit. The weather forecast is looking good for Saturday too. It's all going to be so chic, I can hardly stand it."

Caitlin sounded so cheerful, so *unbothered*. Eve hated her for it.

"Is that all?" she said abruptly.

Caitlin's voice didn't change. "Did you want to talk about something else?"

"No," said Eve, and hung up.

There was nothing on TV. Eve watched a film on her laptop, half an ear to the front door. Chloe and Yelitza came back at about eight-thirty, followed by her mother at nine-thirty. The house gradually quietened, until nothing could be heard but the ticking of the grandfather clock by the front door.

The front door opened shortly after midnight. Eve instantly felt herself relax.

"Daddy, you're back!" she said, jumping up from the position she'd taken up halfway down the stairs. "I was worried about you."

"What are you doing up, Eve?" her father asked as he set down his briefcase and hung up his coat.

"Waiting for you, of course," said Eve happily.

Her father rubbed his hands through his hair. "Shouldn't you be in bed? You have school tomorrow."

"You have work tomorrow and you're up," Eve pointed out. "I'll make us some tea."

He sighed. "Tea sounds great. I don't suppose there's anything to eat?"

"I could boil you an egg?" Eve suggested, glad to be useful.

Cooking wasn't Eve's strong point, but she knew how to do a perfect boiled egg. It was all in the timing. She set the egg carefully in a white china egg cup, then fanned some chopped carrots around the egg cup to look like toast soldiers. Along with the biscuits and juice, her mother had thrown out the bread as well.

"A feast," her father remarked, chinking tea mugs with her.

Eve sat quietly and watched him eat. Questions were tumbling around in her head, but she couldn't make herself speak them out loud.

I have to talk to him, she thought desperately. *I just have to. This might be my only chance.*

Her father wasn't in a talkative mood either. He finished his egg, crunched through his carrots and drained his tea to the last dregs before he looked up at her.

Tell him about Caitlin. Tell him about the shopping centre. "I'm having a great time organizing the party on Saturday," said Eve brightly, trying to ignore the voice in her head. "It's all looking really fantastic."

"That's good."

Eve noticed the dark shadows under her father's eyes. The shopping centre needled at her mind.

"I will always love you no matter what," she blurted. "You know that, don't you?"

He looked weary. "That's good to know, Evie. I don't feel too lovable at the moment."

Eve sensed that he wanted to tell her something. She wished that he would. She stacked his plate and mug in the dishwasher.

"Something's bothering you," her father said behind her. "Isn't it?"

Biting her lip, Eve turned back to face him. Where should she start?

"I went to the shopping centre on Friday night," she said at last, trying to quell her nerves.

He whitened. "What?"

Eve saw that she'd shaken him. "There was a group of us," she rushed on. "We just went to have a look. Is everything OK on the construction site, Daddy?"

"Everything's fine," he began soothingly.

"It's not fine!" Eve felt close to tears. "There are whole walls that haven't been built. Wires everywhere. I thought you said you were doing finishing touches!"

"Please don't worry, Evie," he said, moving towards her and grasping her hands tightly. "There have been a few . . . challenges, but it's nothing I can't handle. I will do whatever it takes to make the shopping centre a success. I would never let you down. You're too precious. You do believe me, don't you?"

His eyes were intent, his hands warm in hers. Eve felt a bit better. She wiped her eyes. "Of course I believe you, Daddy," she said, willing it to be true.

He kissed her on the top of her head. "That's my girl. Now off you go to bed. Heartside High's most beautiful princess needs her sleep."

Eve kissed him back on the cheek gratefully. She wished she could talk to him about Caitlin as well, but she was feeling too tired and fragile for that now.

"I will always love *you*, no matter what," he said unexpectedly. "Remember that."

Eve felt exhausted as she headed up to bed, but calm. Her dad would make everything right with the shopping centre. She wondered if on some level he already knew about the struggles she was having about Caitlin.

He loves me no matter what, she repeated to herself, yawning and climbing the stairs to her room.

The thought was like balm. It made all the difference in the world.

SIXTEEN

The island air was warm, scented with the heavenly smells of spicy grilled chicken as it spat and sizzled over the enormous fire pit behind the swagged, striped marquee. Eve stood among the flares on the beach and watched the party boat approaching across the waves, the lights of Heartside Bay sparkling on the horizon. The butterflies in her stomach were having a party all of their own.

The steel band struck up on the beach beside Eve, making her jump a little. As the light-bedecked boat bumped up gently against the jetty and Eve heard the excited chatter of the guests, she started to relax. Everything was going to be perfect. She adjusted her sea-blue sequinned dress and wiggled her pedicured toes in the cool sand, then lifted her arms and waved as the crowd swept off the boat.

"This place looks awesome!" Ollie gasped, giving Eve a hug. In his surfer shorts and Hawaiian shirt, he looked every inch the beach dude. "Even better than I pictured it when I was here."

"When were you ever here, Ollie?" Lila's pink crop top showed off her long slender body and her flowing skirt brushed the sand, sparkly flip-flops peeping out from underneath. She glanced down, startled as a smiling white-tuxed waiter draped a beautiful orchid lei around her neck. "Oh my goodness, these are so pretty!"

"Lucky distraction," Ollie whispered to Eve as Lila laughed at something the waiter whispered in her ear. "Some things are better kept a secret. I love the band. Show me the dance floor and let's get this party started!"

Polly looked gorgeous wearing a vintage fifties-style dress printed with beach umbrellas, her hair dyed a warm chestnut-brown that brought out her hazel eyes. Rhi wore an emerald-green jumpsuit with her curly hair left loose and natural around her face. Max had opted for tight blue trunks and an open-necked shirt in the style of James Bond. As for Josh, he looked much the same as ever, shirt and jumper and skinny jeans with a battered beach hat on his head.

Eve savoured the awe in her friends' eyes as they took in the beachside scene and started to relax.

I can do this, she thought. *And everyone knows it.*

Adjusting the white orchid in her hair, she moved among the guests, laughing and chatting and encouraging everyone to try the punch: a pineapple and mint combination that she and Caitlin had invented together.

"It's gorgeous, so refreshing. You'll love it."

"Caitlin's just getting off the boat," said Rhi, gently stroking the petals on her orchid lei. "Who's she with?"

Eve steeled herself and turned round.

Caitlin looked stunning in a pearly green mermaid dress, her hair swept gently back from her face, her eyes bright and warm. A tall blonde girl was with her, freckled and laughing beneath a pink straw fedora. They were holding hands.

"Darling," said Caitlin, kissing Eve warmly on both

cheeks. "This all looks too chic. Who is your party planner? You must give me her number."

The girl beside her laughed, and pushed her hat back off her open, friendly face. "Hi, I'm Jessica, Cait's girlfriend," she said, smiling. "It's great to meet you, Eve. Cait's had so much fun planning this with you."

Eve shook Jessica's hand as if she was in a dream. "Have a drink," she found herself saying. "Coats and bags can be left in the marquee. Please excuse me, I have a hundred things to do. . ."

She walked across to a darker, quieter part of the beach and stood there, shaking.

Caitlin was gay.

After a moment, Eve hurried up to a private spot beside the marquee where she could watch the party guests without being seen herself. Her friends were milling around the jetty and the marquee, queuing at the fire pit for barbecued chicken and swaying to the steel band. Eve started to panic. They would see Caitlin with Jessica, they would remember how Eve had kissed Caitlin in that stupid dare at Heartwell Manor. They would see Eve standing at her own party without a date – and they would know.

Everyone would know.

Eve gazed down on the boys, willing herself to fancy someone, to line someone up to flirt with and maybe kiss before the evening was out. As if drawn by a magnet, her eyes kept finding Caitlin and Jessica.

The two girls were sitting by the fire pit, together with Ollie and Polly, Josh and Lila. Everyone was laughing about something, chattering away as if they'd known each other for ages. Ollie took Jessica's hat and put it on his own head. Caitlin looked amazing in her green dress, glittering like an emerald in the firelight.

Eve closed her eyes, struggling to think clearly. Her friends seemed OK about Caitlin and Jessica. They were both beautiful, confident girls. How could they be so open about their sexuality? She felt more envious than ever. She couldn't hide her feelings for much longer. She'd hidden them for such a long time already.

Painting a smile on her face, Eve emerged from the shadows, walking among her guests, smiling and laughing without hearing a single word anyone said to her.

The marquee looked spectacular, the central poles decked out to look like palm trees. Tables and chairs were set out in groups, coconut-shell candles glowing on bright woven tablecloths. People were starting to come inside, plates piled high with barbecued chicken and salad. Mellow reggae music played in here, a different vibe to the pumping beats outside the tent flaps.

"The punch is nearly gone," said a waiter near Eve's ear, making her jump out of her skin. "Shall we start serving the bottled juices?"

"Whoops," said Caitlin, appearing beside the waiter. "I had no idea your friends would drink so much so quickly, Eve darling. I guess it's the sign of a successful party."

Eve felt her composure start to slip. She lifted a finger and pointed hard at Caitlin.

"You were responsible for ordering the drinks. And now look what's happened!"

Caitlin looked surprised. "We have plenty of cold bottled juices and sodas, darling. And anyway, they've started serving the food now. Pineapple and mint is completely gorgeous by itself, but utterly vile alongside barbecued chicken."

"We shouldn't have run out of punch," Eve shouted. She moved closer to Caitlin and poked her in the chest. "It's going to make me look *stupid* if we run out of punch. I can't look stupid at my own party! I knew I should have done this by myself. I can't trust you. I can't trust anyone!"

"Eve," said Caitlin gently. "Slow down. What's going on?"

"You *know* what's going on!" Eve was feeling almost hysterical. "You . . . her . . . punch. . ."

"Goodness me, it sounds like you're challenging me to a duel."

"Don't laugh at me," Eve howled.

"Come on, we need to talk."

Eve felt Caitlin grab her hand and yank her out of the marquee, into the darkness.

"I understand how you're feeling, Eve," said Caitlin in a low voice. "Talk to me. I'm listening."

"I don't want to feel like this," Eve shouted, pummelling at Caitlin, fighting to get away from her. "I want to feel *normal*."

Caitlin wiped the tears from Eve's cheeks. "You'll ruin your make-up with all these tears."

Eve took a deep, shaking breath and composed herself.

"I really do understand," Caitlin said quietly. "Not long ago, I was you."

"You and Jessica. . ."

"We've been together for a couple of months. Jessi is the first person I've felt comfortable with. My first girlfriend." Caitlin giggled. "It sounds so strange. But right too."

"Did you ever . . . date boys?" Eve managed to ask.

Caitlin waved a hand. "Don't go there. Hideous. I tried and tried but it was all a lie. So exhausting."

"I'm so tired of it all," Eve hiccupped.

The tears flowed despite her best efforts. Caitlin put a comforting arm round Eve's waist.

"I liked our kiss," Eve whispered, burying her burning face in Caitlin's shoulder.

"Me too," said Caitlin into her hair. "Don't tell Jessi."

Eve giggled wanly. This was such a strange conversation. "How do you know?" she said at last. "You know, once and for all, if you're. . .?"

Caitlin patted her arm. "One day you will meet someone you fit with," she said simply. "That's when you know."

Eve felt a little happier thinking someone as cool and gorgeous as Caitlin could be gay. And maybe there *were* still boys out there who would fit with her, like Caitlin said. The prospect gave her a little hope.

A strange thought struck her. "Does my dad know about you?"

"Probably," said Caitlin. "I took Jessi to one of my father's parties a month ago. Your dad was there."

I'll always love you no matter what. Could her dad have suspected Eve's confusion? Could he have brought Caitlin into Eve's life for a reason? Eve didn't know whether she felt anxious or relieved at the thought.

"Friends again?" said Caitlin.

It felt really nice, hugging Caitlin. *But just as friends*, Eve reminded herself.

There was a scream of anger down on the beach that made them both turn and look. Lila was nose to nose with Polly.

SEVENTEEN

"Tell me," Lila was hissing in outrage. "How long have you two been seeing each other?"

Ollie was standing in the shadows, looking paralysed. Polly's eyes were wide and haunted. "I swear, we haven't been seeing each other, Lila—"

Lila laughed mirthlessly. "I'm not stupid you know." She looked at Ollie, standing silently in the shadows behind Polly. "Every time I look at you two these days, you're making big cow eyes at each other. Have you been sneaking around behind my back? Tell me!"

Polly came to life. "I would never do that to you, Lila," she said vehemently. "I've seen what happens when people cheat. It just causes misery."

Eve sensed disapproving eyes turning in her direction. She squirmed, thinking about Rhi and Max.

Lila looked at Ollie again. Eve could see that Ollie was avoiding her eye.

"Just hugging, were you? Pull the other one," she said at last.

"It's true!" Polly looked close to tears. "I . . . I do like Ollie but I'd never do anything, I swear—"

"You *like* me?" Ollie interrupted, looking astonished. "But you're always winding me up about how stupid I am."

Polly had turned bright red. "Forget I said anything," she muttered, folding her arms tightly across her body.

Either the firelight was casting a red glow on his cheeks, or Ollie Wright was blushing as vividly as Polly was. He seemed oblivious to Lila's furious glaring.

"You like me?" he repeated. "But . . . I like you too, Polly. I've always liked you but I thought. . ."

He stuttered into red-faced silence. Polly put her hands to her mouth, peeping over the top of her fingers like she'd never seen him before.

"What do you mean, you've *always* liked Polly?"

Lila said, looking more upset than ever. "You've been going out with me for months!"

"You dumped me last week," Ollie pointed out, tearing his eyes from Polly. "Remember?"

Lila gave a choking cry of rage and stormed away down the beach. There was a brief silence, then a storm of chattering.

Everyone loves decent gossip at a party, Eve thought grimly. She realized that she felt sorry for Lila. It was a strange sensation.

She hurried into the darkness after her former enemy, following Lila's footsteps through the sand as they zigzagged erratically across the beach. The last flare was some distance behind her, the moon offering the only light, when Eve at last heard sobbing.

"Are you OK, Lila?" she called, shading her eyes and peering into the gloom."

"Do I sound OK?" Sitting on a sand dune with her knees drawn up to her chest, Lila looked utterly crushed. She peered at Eve with red eyes. "Come to gloat?" she said, wiping her nose.

Maybe it was the conversation she'd just had with Caitlin, but Eve felt as if something inside her had changed. Softened, perhaps.

"No," she said honestly. "Although I understand why you might think that."

She sat beside Lila. Together they watched the white tips of the waves blooming through the darkness, listening to the soft shush of the surf on the shore.

"I did dump him, I guess," Lila sniffed. She glanced sideways at Eve. "Do you think they were seeing each other when Ollie and I were together?"

Eve thought about the hug she'd seen in the shopping centre. She shook her head. "No. Because they care more about you than they do about themselves."

Which is more than can be said for me, she thought.

"Then what if Ollie was pretending I was Polly every time we kissed?" Lila said in despair.

"Are we talking about dented pride or broken hearts here?" Eve asked briskly.

"Pride, I guess," Lila mumbled after a moment.

Eve felt wistful. If only her life was as simple as Lila's. "Then you'll recover just fine," she said. "You and Ollie just didn't work out. It happens. The heart does what it wants, whether we like it or not."

"Well, this heart wants a little fun for a change," said Lila, suddenly sounding decisive. "I'm not going to date anyone for a while."

"Not even Josh?" asked Eve, unable to resist.

Lila looked shocked. "Josh? No! Why do you think I would date Josh?"

"How the world can change," Eve remarked, dusting sand off her dress. "One minute we're at each other's throats and the next you're asking for relationship advice. I'm not the best source of advice just now, believe me."

Lila stared curiously at her. "You're a real surprise sometimes, Eve."

Eve smoothed her hair. "I hope that's a compliment."

"It is." Lila smiled. "Thanks for coming after me. Sitting here instead of queening it around your party. It's a great party, by the way."

"I should have parties more often," Eve mused. "Once a week is about right."

Lila laughed. "You know," she said in wonder, "I never thought we'd be friends."

Eve heard the motor boat before she saw it. Engines revving, lights on full beam, it skidded on to the sand, throwing up a powerful arc of water that quenched three of the beach flares. Eve was on her feet at once, running with Lila back up the beach. She pictured robbers, kidnappers, party crashers. . .

Ryan Jameson leaped off the boat. He stumbled slightly as his feet hit the sand, which spoiled the effect a little. Several people cheered when they recognized him.

"Lila!" Ryan shouted with a flourish, hunting through the crowds. "I've come to claim you. I can't go on like this! I love you!"

Eve felt furious. Who did Ryan think he was, crashing her party so spectacularly? *I'll grind him to dust*, she thought, preparing to go on the attack.

Lila caught her arm. "Wait, Eve. It's OK. I kind of . . . like his style."

Eve didn't like the gleam in Lila's eyes. "Don't tell me Ryan is going to qualify as 'fun'," she said warily.

Lila giggled. "Come on, he makes a decent distraction. Don't you think?"

Ryan had spotted Lila now, and was striding towards her with his arms extended. Eve cringed. How could he be so embarrassing? Didn't he know what a fool he was making of himself? He just didn't know when to stop!

"Lila," Ryan declared, going down gallantly on one knee. The crowd watched, agog. "I can't spend another moment away from you. Kiss me."

"You know how to make an entrance," said Lila, folding her arms and grinning at him. "I'll give you that."

"I want more," Ryan said passionately. "Much more."

Lila rolled her eyes, laughing. "Fine. You want a kiss? I'll give you a kiss."

Ryan looked as if he couldn't believe his ears. "Seriously?"

Lila fluttered her eyelashes. "Get on with it or I might change my mind."

Ryan scrambled to his feet, almost knocking Lila off her feet as he kissed her soundly on the lips. There was a roar of appreciation from the crowd. Ryan pulled away from the embrace and punched the air as if he'd won some kind of kissing trophy.

Eve had had enough. Was she the only person around here who remembered Ryan's idiocy at the shopping centre?

"OK, so now you can leave," she said coldly. "Hop back into your little boat and chug away, Ryan. I recall banning you from this party."

"Give him a break, Eve."

"He nearly gave *you* a break, as I recall," Eve hissed. "Legs, arms, back. Skull. This is my party and I want him to leave."

Ryan puffed out his chest for the benefit of the watching crowd. "This island is public property. I can be here if I want."

Eve wanted to stamp her feet in frustration.

"My security team might have something to say about that," she said sweetly.

Two burly bouncers were heading towards them, talking into their mouthpieces. Ryan leaned towards her, his eyes shining with anger through his fringe. "You're as big a fraud as your father, Eve Somerstown," he said.

For a hideous instant, Eve's entire world stopped turning.

What did he mean?

EIGHTEEN

Eve's first instinct was to stop Ryan from saying any more. The crowd had already started murmuring, looking at each other and wondering. Instinctively, she threw her head back and laughed as loudly and realistically as she could. She'd had plenty of practice at diverting attention in this way. It wasn't difficult.

"You're such a drama queen, Ryan," she said, still laughing. "Whatever do you mean?"

"Everyone knows the construction of the shopping centre has been delayed," Ryan said nastily. "What has Daddy been doing with everyone's money, I wonder?"

Shut up, shut up, shut up. Eve kept her smile pinned in place as her brain clamoured for Ryan's blood.

"You don't understand a thing about business, do

you Ryan?" she said in her most condescending voice. "Why would you? You don't run a multinational business like my father. You're just the kid from the café."

"Stop being so boring, guys," Lila complained. "Is he staying or not, Eve?"

Eve pretended to consider. "Fine," she said, as if it didn't matter to her either way. "He can stay." And she waved at the bouncers, who stopped and headed back the way they had come.

"Now kiss and make up, both of you," said Lila, rolling her eyes. "This is meant to be a *party*."

Eve didn't like the smile Ryan gave her. He knew he'd hit a nerve. As she stepped towards him for a loud air kiss, she hissed into his ear: "Keep your big mouth shut, Ryan, or the police might just find something belonging to you inexplicably lying around in the shopping centre. OK?" Then she stepped back again, her smile firmly in place. "There," she said for Lila's benefit. "Friends. Come on Lila, I want to dance."

Lila slipped her arm through Ryan's. "I think I'll stick with Ryan for a while if you don't mind, Eve."

Eve felt like she'd been punched in the stomach. So much for Lila being her friend now.

"Suit yourself," she said coldly, turning on her heel in the sand.

This is meant to be a party. Lila's words echoed round Eve's head as she moved among her guests alone, her head held high. All of a sudden, she wasn't in the party mood.

"Want to dance, Eve?" said Ollie, jumping around the dance floor like an excitable puppy with his Hawaiian shirt flapping open to his navel.

"If I wanted to dance with a clown, I'd go to the circus," Eve snapped. "You dance like a toddler needing the bathroom."

"Cheers for that, Eve," Ollie said, looking offended. "You really know how to make a guy feel good about himself."

Eve swept on towards the marquee. Nothing ever worked out the way she wanted it to. Nothing ever went right for her. How could Lila act as if she liked Eve one minute, and then choose to hang out with someone who had said such an awful thing about Eve's father?

If it wasn't for my dad, we wouldn't even be HAVING this party, Eve thought savagely. He didn't deserve to have people talking about him behind his back.

You're as big a fraud as your father. . .

Was Ryan right? Was her father a fraud?

Was *she* a fraud?

Fraud. . . Fraud. . .

She nearly bumped into Polly outside the marquee.

"Have you seen Ollie?" asked Polly shyly. "I've lost him."

"You really should keep tabs on that boy," Eve said harshly, pushing past. "He's so shallow he's probably forgotten about you already. You need to hurry up and find him again before he kisses someone else."

Polly looked stricken. "Don't say that."

Everywhere Eve looked, people were getting it together. Talking quietly, their heads close. Dancing with their arms round each other. Kissing. So much *kissing*. The thought of all the romance sickened her. *It was her party*. She wanted to be laughing, holding hands and kissing too. Instead here she was, alone and confused. She was *always* alone.

She stopped dead as she saw yet another couple in a tight embrace. Caitlin's dark head, Jessica's fair one. Jessica's pink hat had fallen off and was lying on the sand at their feet. Eve stared at them in their private bubble of romance, and bit her lip so hard she could taste blood. They made it seem so simple. As if it was nothing at all. She felt more alone than ever.

Tearing her eyes away, she hurried on across the sand. She was climbing on the rocks now, heading for higher ground, away from the crashing surf and the lazy boom of the music. How was she ever going to feel happy again?

A lone figure sat a short distance ahead of her, his long legs folded underneath him, his straw hat pushed to the back of his head and a sketch pad on his lap. Eve felt a rush of hope.

"Hey stranger," she said, sitting down beside him. "Not dancing?"

Josh added some cross-hatching to his lively rendition of the party down below their feet. "I dance like a giraffe on roller skates," he said. "Dangerously. It's better for all concerned if I stay right here."

"The music sounds gorgeous," Eve said as the steel

band echoed on the wind. "Like a Caribbean dream. How would you draw music?"

Josh thought about the question. "Probably as badly as I dance," he said at last.

"Parties aren't really your thing, are they?" Eve asked, looking at him sympathetically.

He looked a little embarrassed. "Honestly? No. But I'm very grateful that you invited me."

Eve nudged him with her arm. "Of course I invited you," she said with a laugh. "I like you, Josh. Don't you get it? I really, really do."

And before she lost her nerve, she removed Josh's hat, put her arms round his neck and kissed him.

NINETEEN

Eve felt Josh freeze. He tentatively returned her kiss, but pulled back almost at once.

"Sorry," he said, flushing bright red. "You kind of took me by surprise."

Eve wanted to die a thousand deaths of humiliation. "It's fine," she said, forcing a laugh. "I just thought I'd give it a try."

"I really am sorry, Eve," he stuttered. "I like you a lot, but . . . just not in that way."

Eve refused to let herself cry. Her mascara could not take much more punishment. "Honestly, Josh, it's fine," she repeated. "It's good for me to know that I'm not entirely irresistible."

She sounded wooden and pathetic. But "you were my last hope" would have sounded a lot worse, she knew.

"That was probably the worst kiss you've ever had," Josh groaned. "I haven't had much practice, you see. Beautiful girls don't jump on me very often. I'm basically an idiot in that department."

Eve found that she was already feeling a bit better. "A very talented idiot," she pointed out.

"Just not at kissing," said Josh gloomily.

"I'm sure you'll be just fine when you find someone that fits."

Eve realized with a little stab of shock that she was echoing Caitlin's words from earlier. She recalled Caitlin's other words from weeks ago, about romance coming and going but friendship remaining. Maybe what she needed right now was a friend.

"You really are beautiful, Eve," said Josh helplessly. "And kind when you want to be. And funny. And you give great parties."

"Parties you don't enjoy," Eve pointed out.

"Parties that are great to draw," Josh corrected, blushing again. "And you are an awesome business partner. Seriously, I'll be your business partner any time you want. I like being with you, even though you ask weird questions about flowers when I'm trying to sketch. It's just—"

"It really is OK, Josh." Eve found that she meant it this time. "I can do friends if you can."

Josh beamed with relief. "I'd love that," he said gratefully.

They sat together in the moonlight for a while, and Eve did her best not to interrupt as Josh shaded in the stripes on the marquee. She found that she was feeling more relaxed than she had all evening.

"Enough," said Josh, folding up his sketch pad. "Do you want to do something else?"

The whole island was on a slope, cliffs at the back and a flat shoreline at the front. Guitar music and laughter were drifting down to Eve from above where she and Josh were sitting, mingling with the mellow tones of the steel band below on the beach. It sounded as if a few guests had split from the main party and were making their own entertainment on the highest point of the island.

"Let's go and see what's happening higher up," Eve suggested.

It was a steep climb. Eve kicked off her jewelled flip-flops and hitched up her dress, grabbing Josh's hand for the steeper parts. The music grew louder and more rhythmic the closer they got to the top.

"Hi, guys!" said Rhi in delight as Eve and Josh scrambled on to the wide, flat plateau at the very top of the island. She laid aside the guitar she was holding.

"Eve was missing me," said Max, grinning beside Rhi in the firelight. "Weren't you?"

"In your dreams, Max," Eve responded. She took in the quiet groups of people perched on the rocks around a flickering camp fire someone had built. "Josh and I thought we'd check out the music up here."

"Be our guests," said Brody Baxter, a tall blond guy who played guitar and sang at the Heartbeat on weekends. He took up the guitar and started strumming it, singing softly. His voice was warm and mellow and echoed off the rocks.

It's beautiful up here, Eve thought, gazing out at the great glittering moonlit sea far below. *So peaceful*. All her troubles seemed a world away. Up here it didn't matter if you were fat or thin, gay or straight, ugly or beautiful, rich or poor. All that mattered was the flickering flames and Brody's voice pouring through the air like cream.

Brody switched to a faster song next, tapping his fingers against the body of his guitar. The sound bounced and echoed around the rocks. Eve found herself starting to sway to the hypnotic rhythm. The crowd clapped and urged Brody on.

"It's a really great party, Eve," said Rhi behind her.

Eve looked round and smiled. "I'm glad you're enjoying it."

Rhi waved down to where the flares glowed along the beach like fireflies. "Looks like we'll have more company in a minute."

Eve saw a stream of people moving away from the beach up the slope towards them, scrambling over the same rocks she and Josh had just climbed, drawn like moths to Brody's singing.

"Dance?" offered Josh, startling her. "I'll try not to kick you off the cliff by mistake."

There was a cliff edge not far from where they were standing, the rocks falling away in a sheer drop fifty feet or more to the sea below. "Fine," Eve laughed. "But we're dancing on the other side of the fire."

Josh wasn't kidding; he was a terrible dancer. But Eve found that she was enjoying herself regardless, twirling around him to a Brody Baxter favourite, *Fast Lane Freak*. Other people joined in, whooping and stamping their feet on the rocky ground.

"We should do this more often, party queen," said Max, snaking his arm around Eve's waist and kissing her on the neck.

Eve pushed him away. "Stick to your girlfriend, Max Holmes," she teased, and whirled away under Josh's flailing arms.

"What are you lame dudes doing up here?"

Ryan had appeared, the usual smirk on his face and his arm around Lila's waist. Eve thought Lila was looking a little bored. Her good mood evaporated.

Why doesn't Ryan just leave? she thought in irritation. *Everyone's tired of him already.*

"Dancing," said Brody Baxter mildly. "Singing. Chilling."

Ryan strutted around the fire, poking at the flames

with the tips of his trainers. "It's kind of early for chilling, don't you think?"

"Let's go back down to the beach, Ryan," said Lila, giving his arm a tug.

Ryan laughed and glanced at the edge of the cliff. "We should do something really wild. Like cliff jumping or something. The uni kids are always doing it."

Eve found herself disliking Ryan even more than she thought possible. "Absolutely not," she said icily. "It's dark – you can't see what's down there. Only someone completely insane would do it, Ryan."

It was the wrong thing to say. Ryan's eyes gleamed in challenge.

"So I'll be the first then, shall I?" he said. "Anyone want to join me?"

"We're just relaxing up here, mate," said Max uneasily.

"Chicken?" said Ryan with a sneer.

"No one's a chicken," said Max, colouring. "We're just having a good time, OK? What's wrong with that?"

"You guys wouldn't know a good time if it bit you on the backsides," said Ryan.

He walked around the fire and peered over the edge of the cliff. Someone gave a little shriek. Eve felt her blood turn to ice as Ryan paced back five steps.

"No," said Josh, starting forward.

Ryan puffed out his chest and winked at his breathless audience. "See you at the bottom, losers," he quipped, blowing a kiss in Lila's direction. "Let it never be forgotten that Ryan Jameson is a legend."

Lila screamed as Ryan broke into a run, jumping away from the cliff edge and into the darkness. His shriek of defiance faded into the night as he fell towards the sea.

"WHOOO!"

TWENTY

Eve rushed to the edge of the cliff, dimly aware that Lila was still screaming. The moonlit sea lapped peacefully at the base of the cliff, fifty feet down. Apart from a few spreading ripples in the water, there was no sign of Ryan.

"Oh my God," said Rhi hysterically. "Is he OK?"

"He's not coming up," said Eve. She could hear her voice trembling.

The music had stopped. All anyone could hear now was the crackling of the campfire. Even the steel band down on the beach had quietened to nothing, as if the musicians sensed that something had just gone horribly wrong.

"He's not coming up," Eve repeated, her voice higher. "He—"

Something appeared in the water far below. A body, bobbing on top of the waves. Ryan lay face down in the sea, unmoving.

Rhi burst into terrified tears and flung her arms around Brody Baxter's neck. More people started screaming. Josh started ripping off his clothes.

"I have to go down there," he said.

"You can't be serious," said Max in astonishment.

"What else do you suggest?" Josh shouted. "He's face down in the water! If the fall didn't kill him, the sea will!"

Eve couldn't tear her eyes from Ryan's body. The way his hair drifted on the water like seaweed.

Josh folded up his glasses and laid them on top of his shirt and trousers. Then he started climbing gingerly down the cliff, holding on to the rocks, stretching with his legs to find footholds with his toes. About five metres down, he stopped.

"I have to jump the rest," he said grimly.

"Be careful!" Eve called in agony.

Josh looked up, his face and long frame ghostly in the moonlight. "It's fine from here, I know the safest place to jump."

There was a splash. Josh bobbed up almost

immediately and struck out towards Ryan, turning him over. Eve could see the way the gash in Ryan's forehead shone black against his pale face. His eyes were closed.

There was a moment of stillness. Eve was aware of everyone clustered around her now, right on the edge of the cliffs, as Josh gave a hopeless cry that echoed around the rocks.

"Ryan. *Ryan!*"

Ryan was dead.

Lights flashed on the top of the police boat, round and round in a haze of blue. Paramedics moved quietly, with none of the urgency Eve had come to expect from watching hospital dramas on TV. There was no rush. No one to save. Just a boy's body to carry away.

There were people all around Eve, talking quietly and holding each other. Eve was numb to everything but the crashing pain in her head and her heart. The flares on the beach had guttered and died; the unattended fire pit glowed and the charred remains of the barbecue scented the air with grease and charcoal.

This must be what hell feels like, she thought.

Ryan hadn't been so different to her. He had wanted

attention. Friends. That was all. And they had pushed him away at every turn, laughed at him and teased him. Shouted at him. Called him stupid and insane. They had as good as pushed him off that cliff themselves.

Dimly she heard her mother in her head.

You're the hostess, darling. It's your job to look after your guests.

There was nothing she could do for Ryan. But perhaps she could help someone else.

Eve stood up slowly, brushing the sand from her dress. Every person she saw was crying. Some were alone. Some were in huddles. She walked up to the solitary grievers, hugging them, talking to them and listening to them cry.

"You'll be going home soon," she said mechanically, over and over again. "You'll feel better in the morning."

Rhi stood at the water's edge, her arms wrapped tightly around herself, gazing out over the sea towards the lights of Heartside Bay.

"How are you doing?" said Eve, slipping her arm around Rhi's waist.

Rhi shook her head. "Not great. I keep thinking about Ruth. And then I feel guilty. It was Ryan who died here tonight, not my sister."

"You're bound to think of Ruth," said Eve. "She was the last person that you lost. Something like this . . . it will bring it all back."

"It's the flashing blue lights," Rhi said flatly. "I keep seeing the police officers on our doorstep, telling us about the car crash." She turned with a sob, burying her head in Eve's shoulder. "Why do people have to die young? Poor Ryan, Eve. He didn't deserve to die."

"No one deserves to die young," Eve said, holding her tightly. "But life doesn't seem to care, does it?"

A little further down the beach Eve saw Josh with his arms tenderly around Lila, stroking her hair as she wept. Eve hadn't cried yet. She was determined to save it for the privacy of her bedroom tonight, when she didn't have to be strong any more.

There was the sound of an approaching motor boat. Eve recalled with a shudder how Ryan had arrived in a similar style. A short time ago Ryan had been alive, and now he was dead. It was almost impossible to process something so enormous.

The motor boat moored at the jetty and a familiar figure jumped out.

"Daddy!" Overwhelmed with relief, Eve stumbled

into her father's embrace.

"Are you all right? Are you hurt?" her father said urgently. "I came the moment I heard the news. Oh princess, I was so worried. . ."

The smell of her father's overcoat against Eve's cheek was strong and reassuring. He was here now and nothing could hurt her. Everything would be OK.

"I need a word with Eve, Henry."

Chief Greg Murray, head of the Heartside police force, was jogging towards them from the police boat.

"It wasn't my fault!" Eve said, stricken. *But it was,* hissed her inner voice. *It was all your fault.*

"Not now, Greg," said Eve's father. "Can't you see how upset she is?"

"I'm sorry, Henry, but it has to be done," said Chief Murray. He glanced towards Lila, still standing with her arms around Josh by the water's edge. "I have a daughter here as well – I know how you feel. But Ryan Jameson also has parents. The sooner we ask our questions, the sooner all this will be over. We need to investigate Ryan's death before these youngsters forget what happened."

I'll never forget what happened, Eve thought, feeling the horror of the moment Ryan jumped all over again.

She felt her father steering her firmly away from the beach, towards the glossy little motor boat idling at the jetty. "If you want to speak to my daughter," he snapped at the Chief of Police, "then you'll have to call her lawyer. She needs to go home at once."

Eve suddenly felt as weak as a paper doll. Her knees had started shaking badly. Delayed shock, she guessed.

"Have it your way, Henry," Chief Murray called after them. "But your refusal to help with our enquiries might end up counting against you."

"I'll live with that," Eve's dad snapped back. He turned back to Eve, his voice gentle again. "It's OK, Evie, we're nearly at the boat. You poor love, you look done in. Everything's going to be fine. I'll sort all of this out for you. You don't have to worry about a thing."

The little boat coasted away from the jetty as her dad took the helm, steering fast and sure towards the lights of the town. Resting against the soft leather seats, Eve buried her face in her hands and burst into tears. She sobbed until her throat felt raw.

Ryan was gone for ever. And there was nothing anyone could do about it.

TWENTY-ONE

People were gathering outside the church in dark suits and black hats. Sunglasses were everywhere, hiding red eyes. The priest stood quietly by the door, talking to a haggard-looking couple in grey and black. Ryan's parents, Eve realized with a lurch. She pictured the laughing pair who had often worked behind the bar at the Heartbeat with their son. They looked twenty years older now.

"I can't do this," Lila blurted. She pushed her sunglasses on top of her head and wiped her red, blotchy eyes. "I think we should go."

Rhi patted Lila wordlessly on the arm.

"It's important to say goodbye," Polly said, in a voice thick with tears.

"We have come this far. We have to pay our respects," said Eve. She was surprised at how steady she sounded.

Lila's eyes were so puffy, she was barely recognizable. Her hair looked lank, and had been scraped back into a tight ponytail that didn't suit her. For once in her life, Lila looked terrible. But Eve couldn't enjoy the fact. She wondered if she'd enjoy anything, ever again.

She smoothed down her black jacket, polished her dark glasses and set them firmly on her carefully made-up face. "Come on," she said, starting to cross the road. "We're going to be late."

People looked at them as they approached the door of the church. Keeping her head high, Eve ignored their glances. Lila, Polly and Rhi trailed behind her like bedraggled ducklings.

"You!"

Eve paused in the threshold of the church door. She took off her sunglasses and looked directly into the tear-filled eyes of Ryan's mother. Determined not to be a coward.

"I'm so sorry for your loss, Mrs Jameson," she said.

"If we could change any of it, we would," Lila sniffed, and blew her nose on a handkerchief.

Mrs Jameson looked almost wild with grief. "You were no friend of his," she hissed. "How dare you come here today?"

"We tried to stop him," Lila cried, "but he wouldn't listen!"

Eve struggled to stay calm as Lila burst into noisy tears. Polly and Rhi stood by helplessly.

The priest moved forward, looking concerned. "Mrs Jameson, perhaps you would like to take your seat? You'll be more comfortable inside the church."

"I want you to leave," spat Ryan's mother, pointing at Eve. "You and your friend with her crocodile tears. You aren't welcome."

She walked stiffly into the church on her silent husband's arm. The priest looked apologetically at Eve, and headed inside as well.

There was a nasty pause. Lila sobbed loudly into her hands.

"What do you think we should do?" said Polly, looking at Eve with wide and hopeless eyes.

Eve took a deep breath. "The important thing is

to respect Ryan's family's wishes," she said. She felt hollow inside. "We've offered our condolences. Ryan's parents don't want them. I think we should do as Mrs Jameson asked."

Lila was crying so hard that Eve could barely hear herself think. "You two go in," she went on, looking at Rhi and Polly. "You'll be fine. The others are in there already. Lila and I will meet you on the beach when it's finished."

She took Lila's arm gently but firmly. Lila allowed herself to be pulled away.

It wasn't far to the beach. Eve was glad of the cold smack of the wind on her cheeks. It helped her think more clearly.

"That was so awful," Lila hiccupped beside Eve as the wind buffeted them. "I hope I never experience anything so bad, ever again."

Eve felt restless. She had summoned every ounce of courage to get to the church, and now she felt – lost. *The service will have started by now,* she thought. It was grim, thinking about Ryan lying inside a coffin at the altar. Part of her was glad not to be there after all.

"Why don't we have our own remembrance service for Ryan here on the beach?" she suggested. "It's nice, thinking that we're doing something at the same time as the church."

Lila wiped her eyes. "I'd like that," she said, sounding a little calmer. "Let's find some pretty stones and shells."

It felt good to be doing something. Moving along the shoreline with her eyes on the sand, searching for stones and shells, Eve thought about Ryan's desperate need to impress people, his love of an audience. His determination to be the most daring person in the room.

We couldn't have stopped him jumping, she realized.

The thought made her feel a little better.

When she had filled her pockets with wet stones and shells of different colours, Eve joined Lila at the water's edge. They arranged their finds to spell Ryan's name in the sand, and then drew a circle around the picture with a piece of wood that Lila had found by the pier. The tide was lapping at the edge of the circle by the time they had finished. But that was OK, Eve realized.

Fitting, somehow.

Goodbye, Ryan, she thought as the waves washed over the memorial they had made. *Sleep well*.

"You never know what's coming around the next corner, do you?" said Lila. The pebbles and stones swirled and disappeared by their feet. "Any of us could be struck down by a speeding car, or get a fatal illness, at any minute."

Eve nodded. "You're right. We think we're so powerful, but we're not."

Lila blew her nose decisively. "If I've learned anything from the worst week of my life, it's this. Life is too short to play it safe. From now on, I'm going to live like every day is my last day on earth. No more caution. I'll do what I want, when I want. Run naked down the pier. Sing out loud on the bus."

"Everyone would think you were mad," Eve said, half-smiling.

Lila smiled back tearfully. "If it makes me happy, that's all that matters."

Eve wondered what it would be like, not caring about consequences. Just caring about being happy.

Rhi and Polly were coming towards them across the

sand.

"How was it?" Eve asked when they reached her and Lila.

"Sad." Rhi's eyes were red. "But good too. There were some nice readings and songs."

"Have you been on the beach the whole time?" Polly asked.

Eve nodded at the remains of their stone-and-shell memorial. "We said goodbye in our own way."

Lila caught Polly by the arm. Polly looked startled by the intent expression on Lila's face.

"I'm sorry about the way I shouted at you," Lila said. "I had no right to do that. You and Ollie have to grab all the happiness you can. I don't want to fight about it. I don't want to fight about anything ever again."

Polly's eyes glimmered. "Thank you, Lila. That means a lot. I never wanted to hurt you. I'm so sorry that I did."

Lila nodded. "I know. I understand now. After all this sadness," she went on, looking round at everyone, "I think it's important that we are all friends. Real friends. Friends who tell each other the truth, and look after each other, and listen to each other, and never judge each other."

"Agreed," said Rhi, wiping her eyes.

"Definitely," said Polly.

If I don't say something now, I may never say it, Eve thought as everyone moved together in a big group hug.

Like Lila, she had just realized a crucial truth.

Life was too short not to live the life she wanted.

It was time to be honest about who she really was.

TWENTY-TWO

"I have something I want to say to all of you," said Eve.

"You look scared," said Lila, looking at Eve in surprise. "I didn't think you ever got scared, Eve."

Keep going, Eve thought to herself. She swallowed hard. "I have been having a few . . . problems lately," she said, fumbling for the words. "Facing things. About myself."

Her friends were listening now. Eve felt more scared than ever.

"What Lila said about being honest with each other," she hurried on. "I want to be honest with you. You've probably noticed I've been kind of . . . angry lately. Preoccupied. Remember when you saw me a few weeks ago coming out of Ms Andrews' office, Rhi?"

Polly started at the mention of her mother's partner.

Rhi nodded. "I remember," she said. "What about it?"

Eve ploughed on. "I'd been talking to her about something personal. Something that had been troubling me for a while."

"Go on," said Polly encouragingly.

Eve felt like she was beside Ryan, jumping off that terrible cliff. It was a long way down. There was no way of knowing if she'd come up again.

"I think I might be gay," she blurted out.

Lila's mouth fell open.

"What?" said Rhi in astonishment.

"I might not be," Eve hurried on. "My feelings are all over the place at the moment, to be honest. But I have . . . these dreams, and I don't seem to have much luck with boys, not long-term. And then Caitlin came along. You saw me kiss her. I enjoyed it. More than I've ever enjoyed kissing boys. And I've kissed a lot of boys," she added, a little wryly.

"You're telling me," Lila said, recovering. "Wow, Eve. This is big."

I won't cry, Eve thought in determination. "Like I

say, I might not be," she said lamely. "But I think that I probably am."

She stood there, wringing her hands and watching her friends' faces. What would they think? Had she just made the biggest mistake of her life?

"Wow," Lila said again.

"Well," said Polly firmly, "I think it's great. Well done, Eve. I'm so glad you told us."

It was taking Eve a lot of effort to hold it together. "You are?" she whispered, flushing. "You don't think it's weird?"

"I'm hardly going to," said Polly, grinning. "Am I?"

Eve felt Polly's arms come around her and squeeze her tightly.

"That was really brave," Polly said, releasing her. She looked at the others. "Don't you think that was brave, guys?"

"I don't know what to think," Lila said weakly.

Eve realized that Rhi was glaring at her.

"Typical Eve," she said, her eyes sparking with anger. "Making Ryan's death all about you."

Eve flinched. "I didn't mean it that way," she said, feeling a little horrified.

Rhi turned to the others. "Can't you see what she's doing?" she demanded. "She can't bear not being the centre of attention. You stole my boyfriend, Eve, and yet somehow now you're telling me you're gay as if that excuses you for everything you've ever done? You've done some low things in your time, but this is the lowest!"

She hurried away, her arms wrapped tightly around herself and her head down.

"Rhi!" Eve called hopelessly. "Come back! Talk to me!"

But Rhi didn't look round.

It isn't supposed to be this way! Eve wanted to shout after her former best friend. *I didn't choose to feel like this!*

She felt a hand on her arm.

"Rhi will get used to the idea," Polly said. "Give her time."

Lila still hadn't said anything other than "Wow". Now she was staring at her feet, twisting the toe of her shoe into the sand.

Eve suddenly wanted to be by herself.

"You two should go after Rhi," she said.

"What about you?" said Polly in surprise.

Eve started walking towards the pier. "I want to be by myself," she said over her shoulder.

She didn't look back until she had reached the sea wall. Rhi and Polly were already specks in the distance. Eve shivered, and rubbed at her arms. The wind was bitter.

You've said it now, she thought. *And it can't be unsaid.*

How did she feel? Alone, that was for sure. Lighter, maybe. Even with Rhi reacting the way she had, and Lila not looking at her. . . Yes. Lighter was the word. It was as if she had been carrying something heavy on her back for weeks. Months. And now she'd put it down.

Eve rested her back against the sea wall and gazed away from the sea towards the town. Heartside Bay looked just as it always did. Rooftops huddled together along the curving shoreline. Boats bobbing in the harbour, gulls wheeling through the sky with their harsh screams. And yet it was completely different too.

She had never realized how much she was hurting herself by keeping her feelings a secret. Even from herself. The relief was indescribable.

Someone was coming towards her across the beach. With a shock of recognition, Eve saw that it was Caitlin.

"Hey," said Caitlin, coming to a halt in front of her. "Are you OK? Polly just sent me a text."

Eve wrapped her arms more tightly around herself. "What did she say?"

Caitlin's smile was blinding. "That you just did the deed and came out. And that you probably needed a friend right now."

Eve pulled a face. "I just told my friends to get lost," she said.

"Are you going to tell me to do the same?" Caitlin enquired.

"Of course not," Eve said, smiling slightly. "You're one of just two people I know in the entire world who understands what this feels like."

Caitlin gave her a hug. "I'm so proud of you," she said warmly. "I know exactly how difficult that must have been."

Eve clung to Caitlin gratefully. "I feel pretty alone right now," she confessed, pulling back. "Do you promise this gets better?"

"Of course it does," said Caitlin, rubbing her back. "Your friends will come round to the idea. And if they don't, they aren't really your friends at all. Are they?"

Even though Eve felt as vulnerable as a crab without its shell, she took comfort from Caitlin's words. Friendship wasn't friendship if it didn't accept all of you, exactly as you were, warts and all.

She turned her face to the wind, feeling the spray on her cheeks, and thought of Ryan.

I'm still here, she thought gratefully. *I hope I never forget how lucky I am.*

Life, she knew, would never be the same again.